STORM

Retribution

Pamela Cowan

Copyright Page

Storm Retribution is a work of fiction. Names, characters, places and incidents are the products of the author's imagination. Any resemblance to actual events, locales, or persons living or dead, is coincidental.

Windtree
Press

818 SW 3rd Avenue, #221-2218
Portland, OR 97204-2405
855-649-0821

DEDICATION

For Adam and Tracy Fox for their vast
knowledge of the best places to hide a body.

ACKNOWLEDGMENTS

Thank you, first and foremost, to my readers. If you've enjoyed this book I'd love to hear about it. Please visit my website at www.pamelacowan.com.

Thank you to my family for their unwavering support, to my street team, Pam's Peeps, for getting the word out, and to my publisher Maggie Lynch, who continues to believe in and encourage my efforts, and especially to James McCracken and Rose St. Martin Reis. Without their time and efforts this book would not exist.

Finally, thank you to the late Larry Hughes, Solo Angeles Club de Motociclistas (English: Solo Angels Motorcycle Club) an outlaw motorcycle club formed in Tijuana, Mexico in 1959. The club does an annual charity run where they deliver toys to poor children in Tijuana.

BOOKS BY THIS AUTHOR

Vigilante Justice
Storm Justice
Storm Vengeance
Storm Retribution

Mystery & Suspense
Something In The Dark
Cold Kill

CHAPTER ONE

MIRROR LAKE LODGE was bigger than Storm had expected, two stories, timber built, and cedar sided. Though it had obviously been designed to blend into the surroundings, it had too much presence to disappear into the background, even here, among a forest of giant redwoods that swept down a series of hills to the immensity of the Pacific Ocean.

After a quick drive-by they'd parked the car and walked through the dense woods, working their way, sometimes more noisily than she'd have liked, toward the rear of the lodge.

Storm's eyes had adjusted to the dark and she no longer needed to use her cell phone's flashlight. The narrow deer trail they'd followed through the brush opened onto a small meadow surrounded by trees. Damp ferns threw shadows like rows of jagged teeth, and moss hung in tattered green curtains from wind-twisted branches. It was quiet, not even the piping of a frog or the chirping of a cricket to remind you there was something else alive out there.

Looking to her left she could barely make out the shadow that was her father. His presence added to the surreal feeling of the night. She moved forward, pushing through underbrush and past trees until she could see down the long slope to the lodge her mother ran as a bed and breakfast.

Storm could neither see nor hear the ocean, less than a mile away, but its proximity was obvious. For one thing, she could smell it, the tangy mix of salt, seaweed and dead things was unmistakable. Another sign were the colorful floats hanging from the back-deck rail. A row of welcoming yellow porch lights made the green, orange, and blue floats glow. The same light called attention to the back door, the only barrier between her and the mother she hadn't seen in twenty years. A grim smile crossed her lips as she recognized the irony, that the parent she most wanted to see was not the one standing beside her.

From the front of the house Storm heard a door slam and then footsteps on gravel. She stepped back, making sure she was hidden from view. Checking her father, she noted that he'd dropped into a crouch, well concealed by a clump of brush and ferns. She nodded her approval.

They'd acted just in time. The figure of a man appeared from around the front corner of the building, walking steadily across the lawn at the bottom of the slope to her left, moving away from the lodge. Storm watched the red tip of the cigarette he held clenched in his teeth bob up and down. Then she heard a new sound, the rattling of chains.

Searching for the source of the noise, she eventually made out the shape of a dog, a pit bull she thought, chained to a tree. Four trees, their slender trunks covered with distinctive white bark, grew in a loose cluster between the lodge and the line of evergreens that marked the edge of the forest. Their lower branches swept nearly to the ground, partly obscuring her view.

Once she knew what to look for, she soon spotted a second dog and then a third. Three dogs! They'd been lucky they'd stopped when they had. A few more steps and the dogs would have seen or smelled them and barked their heads off, alarming everyone in the house. In fact, Storm questioned why the dogs hadn't barked already. Surely they'd seen the man and should be howling a greeting.

But the dogs didn't bark. Instead, they growled, a low vibration deep in their throats. A sound filled with hate and intention. Straining against the chains that held them, the weak light made their teeth gleam, turned their eyes into luminous green embers. The two dogs were vicious, malevolent. The third dog remained where it had been lying, curled at the base of the tree where it was tied.

The man dropped something he'd been carrying. It crackled when it hit the ground and Storm realized it was a bag of dog food. However, instead of feeding the dogs the man stepped toward the one that hadn't moved. She watched as he nudged it with the toe of his shoe. When it didn't react she assumed it was dead. She was surprised to see the man draw back his foot and kick it. She heard a whimper and the dog seemed to grow even smaller. It wasn't dead, she realized, just terrified.

She heard the man say something, but she couldn't make out what it was. Then she saw the glow of the cigarette grow brighter as he took a deep draw. He took it from between his lips and bent over the dog.

Storm's gun was in her hand.

Bang! Bang! Bang!

The sound blended into one long thundering, pulsing beat.

They ran.

With the sound of the three tightly-spaced shots still echoing, Storm and her father ran the way they'd come. Stumbling over ferns, tearing their pants and the skin of their ankles on grasping blackberry vines, they managed to reach the narrow deer trail. Storm dragged her cell phone from her back pocket, found the flashlight icon and thumbed it on. The light turned the trail white, the brush gray. Storm had never been so grateful for anything. Behind them from the lodge came the sound of a door slamming open, men shouting.

They ran faster, slipping and sliding down the hill until they reached the road. Storm raced toward where she thought she'd left the car. The crunch of gravel underfoot sounded like a challenge she didn't want to make.

The already feeble light seemed to dim as shadows slid across the face of the moon.

"Where is it? I can't find the damn car," Storm whispered.

"There," her father said. "Look there."

Storm looked where he pointed and saw a gleam of metal. It was her car, right where she'd left it, backed in between trees and vicious blackberry vines. She didn't bother with finding a trail, just crashed through the brush, digging the keys from her pocket as she went. She'd left the car unlocked and now she jerked the door open, jumped in, and slid the key into the ignition in one graceful motion.

She started the car as her father dropped into the passenger seat, and tugged his door closed. Leaving the lights off, she drove forward slowly until they were out of the brush and on the level surface of the road, then she slammed her foot on the gas. The tires spun for a moment, then found traction and they shot away.

"What the hell was that?" Her father demanded as she flipped on the headlights. "Why did you shoot that man?"

"He was going to hurt the dog!"

"A dog?" he said, his voice filled with disbelief. "You shot him over a dog."

"Yes, and I'd do it again. I couldn't let—"

Her response was interrupted by the sound of motorcycles. The noise of the unmuffled engines throbbed through the woods. Storm grasped the wheel, fighting as the car slid around a curve at fifty miles per hour, then she braked just making the turn onto North Bank Road. Moving too fast, the tires skittered across the loose gravel and the car slid sideways toward the river. Storm steered into the skid and the car lurched then straightened, picking up speed again.

"You're leaving a dust trail," Storm's father shouted.

"I know," she yelled back. Then they were hurtling across the wooden bridge, their tires sending up a hollow thrum as they passed over the wide wooden planks and the empty places in between.

"Better?" she asked, as the car left the bridge with a jolt then smoothed out on the paved asphalt street.

Twisting in his seat to look out the back window, he said. "Yeah, better. But they aren't far behind."

Ahead in the distance, Storm saw the glow of light in the sky that indicated a city or town. She took the first street that seemed to head in that direction. After a few moments, they saw a house, then another. Soon they were in a residential area, with a posted speed limit of twenty-five. Storm let her speed drop to thirty. Even then she was nervous that at any moment she'd see flashing lights behind.

Cruising deeper into the neighborhood, Storm finally spotted what she'd been searching for, a dark street with too few driveways. Row of cars were parallel parked along the street. She found a spot between two of them, executed a perfect maneuver that put the car's tires inches from the curb, then jumped out. "Come on," she urged, and didn't bother waiting to see if her father followed. If she'd learned anything in the few hours spent with him, it was that he knew when to stay quiet and when to move.

Move was just what they did, jogging quickly, side by side across a lawn toward a carport at the side of a ranch-style house. A bronze minivan took up one half of the space, the rest was filled with stacked firewood.

As they sidestepped alongside the van Storm realized the sound of the motorcycles was getting louder. As her father sidled along behind her his hip bumped into the stack of wood and something shifted. There was a small thud as one of the logs fell loose and hit the ground. Joe hissed a soft curse under his breath. Both froze.

The motorcycles were close. Backing into the small area between the front of the van and the rear wall, Storm stumbled on the short log that had fallen but managed to stay on her feet. The space was very dark, but she didn't dare chance a light. Instead, she hunched down, and waited. She didn't have to wait long before two motorcycles roared past and kept going. They hadn't even slowed.

"They didn't recognize your car," her father said unnecessarily.

Storm nodded. "We got lucky."

"We should wait awhile though."

"Yes," she agreed. She could hear him breathing, shallow, panting breaths that reminded her that he was not young. He'd been thirty-five when he went to prison. That would make him fifty-five now. Not exactly ancient but no, definitely not young.

"At least we can be comfortable." Joe reached up, felt around in the dark, tugged a log free from the pile and set it on end at the front of the van.

"Be careful," she warned. "Don't bump the van. It probably has an alarm."

"Yeah, didn't think about that. But here, have a seat," he whispered. He removed another log and set it near the first. Storm slid the gun into its holster and did as he asked. They sat in tense silence, listening for the sound of the motorcycles, each lost in thought.

Storm hunched forward, elbows on her knees, face resting on her palms, eyes closed. She'd shot a man. Bikers were looking for them. Her husband was probably going to leave her. How had so many things gone wrong in such a short time?

CHAPTER TWO

IT WAS HARD TO BELIEVE that only a few hours had passed since she'd heard the knock on the front door. She remembered thinking it was probably Alex or Grace, or both. Alex and Grace Goodenough were next door neighbors. Retired professors, they now devoted their time to travel. She expected them back from their latest trip to Europe any day and knew they'd be by to pick up their mail and share their latest adventures. Normally Storm looked forward to seeing them, she just wished their timing was better.

The smell of slightly charred burgers and sesame buns toasting on the barbecue grill, had followed her through the house. Her stomach growled. With the kids attending a birthday party at a neighbor's, she'd been looking forward to a quiet dinner with Tom. They were going to talk about the upcoming move to New Mexico. Storm reminded herself that one of her goals was to learn to handle change better, to be a little less OCD, so she amped up her smile, tugged the long sleeves of her Oregon Ducks t-shirt down to hide the scars on her wrist, and opened the door.

He was standing on the porch, literally hat in hand, and he was crushing the life out of it. His hair was cut as short as she remembered, but it was completely gray. His face was pale, with new wrinkles and a scar on his chin she didn't recall. He was still tall, if a little stooped, slender, if a little soft in the middle. Still, even with the changes brought on by two decades in prison, she'd recognize him anywhere. Joe Don Dean, the main character of her nightmares, and the man she'd loved like no other—her father.

She knew she should say something, but nothing came to her. She'd rehearsed this moment ever since learning that her father was due for release. She couldn't remember a thing she'd planned to say. None of it. Maybe if she took a deep breath. She gasped, realizing that for a moment she'd forgotten to breathe. That hadn't been in the rehearsal. Neither had the tornado of pain and conflict that tore through her, ripping at her core, threatening to tear her defenses down to let out something—a roar of pain, tears?

"Why?" Was all she managed.

"Your mother's in trouble and I need your help."

These words might have been the only ones able to stop the torrent of whatever had wound itself so deeply in Storm's stomach that it felt like something alive, something slippery and heavy and coiled to strike. Instead of letting loose a tirade of angry words she responded to his anxious tone and said, "What kind of trouble?"

"I need to borrow your car, maybe a few bucks. You'll get them back."

"I asked you what kind of trouble."

He looked at her—into her eyes—for the first time. His eyes were the color of burnt caramel, like hers, with gold flecks, like hers.

Down the street a door slammed, a skateboard rumbled down a sidewalk, and a dog barked, reminding her that they were still standing on the porch.

She did not want to talk to him out here, in front of the whole neighborhood. Though it was the last thing she thought she'd ever do she said, "Come in," in. Her voice was so absent of emotion it sounded strangely robotic, even to her. "My husband is out back barbecuing. I'd be more comfortable if we went back there." She led him through the house as if he were someone familiar, and he was, wasn't he?

Tom had set their plates on the picnic table and was sitting in front of his, waiting for her. He looked up when he heard her step on the back porch. She moved into the sunlight and shot him a warning look. Then she moved aside as her father stepped from the house and stood beside her. A shiver played up and down her spine as she introduced them, "Tom, this is my father, Joe. Joe, this is my husband, Tom."

Tom stood, extricated himself from the table and stepped back from it, as if he needed a clear space in which to greet this stranger he knew too much about. Her father put his hat on as if to free his hands but made no move to shake. Other than a small nod, he kept his head down, his gaze on the ground. Still a prisoner, compliant and submissive thought Storm. It annoyed her. She bit her lip. Funny, a moment ago she could have dreamed of nothing better than to have her father in front of her, beaten, broken. But now it just pissed her off.

It was Tom who moved forward, stepped across the patio with a measured stride, climbed two of the three steps and put his hand out. "Nice to meet you," was the strange thing he said. Then, as Storm analyzed it, she realized there was nothing else he could say. The polite, expected greeting was better than Tom punching her father—wasn't it? In any case, Tom was relying on his innate good manners and waiting for a cue from her. But what did she want him to do?

"Are you hungry?" she asked. "Tom always makes too much." Courtesy seemed to be the tool by which they were all going to navigate this awkward moment.

"No but thank you. I'm not here to put you out."

"Well, take a seat at least. It's awkward to talk when we're on different levels."

Hesitantly he took the backpack he'd been carrying slung over one shoulder and set it down on the stone patio, then took a seat on a folding lawn chair at the end of the picnic table. He sat perched on the edge as if he were afraid the chair would not bear his weight. Storm took her customary seat at the picnic table and was surprised when Tom stood behind her, his hand on her shoulder rather than taking his own seat.

"So," she said, addressing her father, "please tell me what's wrong. Why does my mother need help?"

He leaned forward in the chair, his forearms resting on his knees, his hands moving constantly in a washing motion, as if they hurt, or as if he could not be entirely still. "Not sure where to begin." He paused a moment, then looked up. "About ten years ago I sent a letter to your Aunt June asking about you and your mother. She wrote me back, said Lisa was well, had inherited a bed and breakfast. That you were married, still living in Beaverton and that I was a grandfather. After that we kept in touch, exchanging letters, writing each other about once a month until she passed on."

Storm experienced the familiar touch of sadness she always felt when something reminded her of her deceased Great Aunt June, the woman who had taken her in when she was thirteen.

Her father continued. "I couldn't stand not knowing how you and your family were doing. so I finally manned up and asked my friend, Rip, who had just been released and owed me a favor, to call your mother. But she wasn't there and he ended up talking to a woman named Jackie. Rip told me Jackie didn't think Lisa was ready to hear from me. However, she said she'd be happy to work as an intermediary and share what she learned about you and your kids, because she understood the importance of family.

Storm could see he wanted her to say something, maybe to ask a question, make this conversation easier, but there was nothing in her DNA, or in their past, that would make her want to make things easier for him.

"After that I managed to get Rip to call once in a while. He only called on Monday's because we knew your mother wouldn't be there. Jackie said she did her errands that day.

"That's how I kept track of all of you. Your mother would tell Jackie, and Jackie would tell Rip and he would write me a letter. I know it sounds strange, but that's what I did.

"I hope you've come to forgive your mother for leaving you while you were in the hospital. I also hope you're willing to help her. After what happened, she had a breakdown and ended up on the street."

"I know what happened to Mom. I got a letter from Aunt June after she died, explaining that she'd wanted to tell me about my mom, but she'd made a promise not to. However, she knew she was running out of time to tell me the truth and decided she had to break the promise and tell me where my mother was, and why I had to stay with Aunt June even though Mom was doing better. That they had decided I needed the stability of Aunt June to get past my past. I know they made the right decision. I'm not sure where I'd be without my aunt. She stepped in for both of you. Did what you should have done."

"That's for sure," Joe agreed. "I'm grateful to her every day. The older I get the more I realize how little I was prepared for a wife, let alone a family. I guess that sounds like I'm trying to make excuses. I don't mean to. I don't know how else to say it. "

Storm was done. She had no interest in rehashing the past. If he wanted to continue walking down memory lane he would be walking alone. Storm shrugged, dismissing him, "Let's just talk about now. What's going on? Why do you think my mother needs help?"

"I called the lodge yesterday. Jackie said four men with motorcycles showed up and moved in. Rough types. Her words, not mine. She said Lisa refuses to kick them out and she thinks it's because she's afraid of them. She thinks maybe they threatened her. Jackie wanted to call the police, but your mother made her promise she wouldn't. Told her she was being silly and that they were paying customers."

"Sounds like Jackie's a bit of a Nervous Nellie," said Storm. Tom's hand on her shoulder was distracting and she wished he'd sit down.

"She's never struck me that way," her father said. "In fact, I'm pretty sure her past hasn't exactly been a bed of roses. Jackie says they pretend to be guests but she's sure they're pressuring your mother in some way. Her wildest guess was that Lisa hired them to protect her. She'd heard I'd been released. I guess the prison sent her a letter?"

Storm nodded. She too had received a letter informing her of the release of Joe Don Dean. She remembered looking at it and wondering what it meant to her. Mostly because she had yet to deal with her anger toward him and wondered what she'd do if he showed up on her doorstep. At least she didn't have to wonder about that anymore.

How had her mother reacted to finding out her ex was getting out of prison? Had she been afraid? Were there things about her leaving that Storm didn't know about? And, if her mother *was* scared, was she justified in her fear? If so, wouldn't helping her father get to her be exactly the wrong thing to do?

She had no answers, just a growing sense of guilt that some of this was her fault. After all, if she'd been brave enough to contact her mother when she first found out where she was, she might now have a relationship with her, some connection beyond the memorized phone number to a bed and breakfast in California. It was a little pathetic.

Finally, she said, "I'm not sure what to think about this. I want to help her but I'm not sure you do. I don't know you."

Her father winced as if she'd slapped him. "I know," he said. "I know and I'm very ashamed of that fact. More ashamed of that than anything, and I have a long list of things to be ashamed of." He stared down at the ground between his feet in that same submissive pose that seemed to come so naturally to him.

It set Storm's teeth on edge and put her somewhere between the conflicting desires of shooting him or patting him on the shoulder reassuringly.

"Once I got out I planned to write you, maybe send a postcard," he continued. "I wanted to let you know I'd like to see you, tell you how sorry I am. I was going to follow that up with a phone call, but now everything has changed. Now I don't have time to take my time. Now I feel like the most important thing is helping your mother. I can't explain why, but I know she's in trouble. I just know it."

"And somehow you think you're the one to charge in, play hero and fix everything?" asked Storm, not trying to hide the sarcasm in her tone. She felt Tom's hand tighten on her shoulder.

"I don't know about that," he said. "Once I get there I may have to call out the troops, get the police involved, but I have to scope it out first. That's all I'm asking from you, help me get out there and see what there is to see. We're the only family your mother has. I promise I'll return your car as soon as I figure it out. I'll get you your money back as soon as I get some work."

Tom's fingers tightened even more. Storm shifted away from the bruising pressure, surprised by the strength of his grip but more so by his next words.

"It's time for you to go."

She twisted in her seat and looked up at him. "What?" she asked.

"It's time for your father to go," he said. He stepped around the table and walked up the porch steps. "Here, let me get the door for you," he said, swinging it open.

"Tom, what are you doing?" Storm asked.

"It should be obvious. I'm kicking your father out of our house."

"But—but, we were talking."

"Talking's over. I have been very patient, but my patience has worn out." He gestured toward the door. "Would you like to escort your father through the house and back out the way he came in, or should I?

Storm was so shocked by the no-nonsense command from her normally gentle husband that she couldn't react.

Joe stood, absently touched his forehead with two fingers, a sort of unconscious salute. Then he headed up the stairs and walked past Tom through the door and into the house without looking up.

Storm followed him down the hall and into the living room, then darted past him to open the front door. When they were outside, she turned to him and said, "He shouldn't have—"

"Don't be upset with him," he said, interrupting her. "In his shoes, I'd have done the same. He's got to protect you. It's his job. The same way I've got to try and protect your mother."

"I know," said Storm. "But both of you need to understand that I never let anyone tell me what I can or cannot do. Even if it is to protect me."

Maybe it was the presence of her father, but the words rang in her ears with the angry, petulant tone of a child.

"If there was something I could do, or say, to show how much I regret that night," he told her. "How I would give anything to have a time machine, so I could go back—"

This time it was her turn to interrupt. "Do you have a number where I can reach you?"

He shook his head, "No, I'm sorry. I don't have the money to get one. The halfway house has a landline, but I don't plan to go back right away."

"You're still going to see if you can help Mom? How are you going to get there?"

He held up his fist, thumb extended. "I may not be up on all the current technology, but I'm pretty sure this thing still works. I'm going to walk to the highway and see if I can thumb a ride."

"How long do you think it will take you to get to Crescent City that way?"

"Not sure. If I'm lucky and catch a ride straight through, seven or eight hours.

"And a whole lot more if you're not lucky."

"I can't argue with that," he said. "But I still have to go."

Storm nodded and moved aside, then watched as he lifted his battered bookbag to his shoulder and left, his long strides moving him down the sidewalk quickly.

Storm stepped into the house and shut the door. For the barest moment she leaned back against it. Then, after a deep, steadying breath, she forced herself to move.

Tom was not in sight, so she went to their bedroom, where she dragged a small carry-on bag from the closet and began filling it. She moved quickly, tossing in jeans and a couple of black, long sleeved jerseys, a flannel shirt in case it was cold, a pair of black slacks and a white blouse that had proven to be fairly wrinkle resistant. She added a pair of flats. The running shoes she had on would do for casual wear. In the bathroom, she gathered a few more things, including one of the travel-sized toothpastes, her dental hygienist gave her every six months.

What the hell was she doing?

Her rational side, silently observing as she packed, now came to the fore. *Are you really going to run off on some heroic mission to save your mother?* The question was full of self-mockery. *This is the woman who ran away, abandoned you.*

Storm, who had been born Willow but had legally changed her name, felt like she was standing in two different times and in two different bodies. There was Storm, the adult, who hated her childhood and her parents. Then there was Willow, the child, who remembered a mother who baked oatmeal cookies but refused to add raisins, joking that they were dead grapes and they weren't grape cannibals. The mother who had helped tie her sneakers with double knots, so they wouldn't come undone, so the other kids wouldn't find out she didn't know how to tie them by herself yet. This was her mother, damn it, and no matter what she'd done that meant something. She was going.

Storm was as shocked by this as Tom would be when he found out. It was so unlike the person she'd tried to become. That woman's life had been predictable and run on a tight schedule of appointments with dentists, doctors and hairdressers. A calendar filled with all the little tasks like planning meals, buying groceries, sweeping the patios and trimming the roses. She'd been so organized. Never missed a birthday, sent cards at Christmas.

Then again, it had been some time since she'd been that woman. Everything had changed and she knew exactly when.

She hadn't quit her job yet. She'd still been working as a probation officer. That morning she'd been in her office talking to one of her clients about a story in the paper. Everyone had been talking about it, the article had concerned a local man who had abused his children in a horrific way but due to a glitch, had been released. They'd talked about justice and he'd promised to deliver it—with her help. After that had come late nights, missed appointments, forgotten errands, lies. She had become someone else yet again. Not a mother, or wife. Not a probation officer, but a vigilante. Before that change she'd never have dreamed of leaving Tom and the kids while she went off to—"

"Stormy."

Tom's voice, calling from the kitchen, broke her chain of thought. Zipping the bag shut, Storm left it on the bed and went to talk to him.

"Did you still want to eat?" he asked. He was holding their dinner plates.

"No," she told him. "I'm not hungry."

He tossed the paper plates and the untouched food into the garbage. Then he leaned back against the counter and looked at her. He said nothing for a moment, obviously waiting for her to start what would undoubtedly be a tough conversation. Only, she didn't know where to start.

"Well?" he finally said.

"Well, I guess, I mean, I was surprised. I couldn't believe you'd kick someone—kick my father—out of the house."

"What's not to believe?" he asked a deep furrow forming between his eyes. "That the person responsible for the scars on your body, the scars in your mind . . . How could you think that—that man— would be welcome in our home?"

"I didn't say you were wrong. I said I was surprised. You have every right to be annoyed. He is the reason for all the things you just said—all the awful things I do, the awful way I look."

"There is nothing wrong with the way you look, goddamn it, or anything you do, for that matter. But that's exactly what I can't stand. The way your childhood messed with your head, with your belief in who you are. I can't help but hate him for that."

"I know. I get it. I hate him for that too. Believe me. But I . . . well I can't explain it, other than to say, he is my father, no matter what else. That's the final truth, right? I didn't get to choose him and I didn't get to choose my mother. But that's who they are and if my mother's in trouble, if this person, this Jackie he talked to is right, and she needs help then—"

"Then she should call the police like any normal person would. If she doesn't, then she's probably involved in something illegal, right? She's no better than he is. You're right, you didn't get to choose them, but you can choose not to have them in your life. You can choose not to help them. Your parents are a perfect pair. They both left you when you needed them the most. Why in the world would you want to do anything for either one of them? Damn it, Stormy, you know I love you, but I'm putting my foot down. I will not let you loan that man your car or give him a dime."

Storm felt a hot curl of anger ripple through her, every nerve ending coming alive as he spoke. With a smile she knew looked a little bit crazy she said softly, "You don't tell me what to do. No one tells me what to do."

"I'm just trying to protec—"

"Control. The word you want is control. That's not going to happen. But you're right, I'm not going to loan my father my car, or give him money. Instead, I'm going to drive to California and find out what's going on, and I'm leaving right now!"

Before she could change her mind, before Tom's wounded expression tore her nerve away, Storm strode from the kitchen, slowing only long enough to grab her bag from the bedroom. She was sure Tom would follow her, try to stop her. When he didn't she was somewhat dismayed, but she couldn't stop. Not until she found out her mother was safe. It didn't make sense. It wasn't logical. But she was doing it anyway.

CHAPTER THREE

HE WAS WALKING ALONG the side of the road, his pace fast, his eyes focused on the distance ahead. She drove past, went two blocks, slowed.

"Damn it," she muttered under her breath. This was the man who had dragged her into his lap, doused her with rum, and then purposefully lit his lighter. This was the man who, instead of coming to visit his daughter in the burn unit, stayed drunk, drove drunk, hit an innocent girl walking home from school and went to prison for it.

She sighed. In a way, none of it mattered. He was still her father and there was nothing she could do about it. Reluctantly she pulled over and unlocked the door.

He stepped up to the car and bent to look in at her, one eyebrow going up, a question he didn't ask. Then he got in.

She drove a short distance and pulled into the familiar parking lot of a neighborhood grocery store. She chose a spot at the front, close to the ice dispenser and can return.

A woman was returning empty soda cans. When Storm's daughter, Lindsey, was younger she'd decided a friendly giant lived inside the can return machine. She'd loved nothing better than listening to the satisfying crunch as the giant chomped through his dinner.

Storm sighed again. "We should go in and get some supplies for the trip."

He said nothing, only nodded, got out and followed her inside. She pulled a cart free "Find something to eat and drink. We don't want to have to stop once we get rolling. I have almost a full tank of gas. We'll get more when we need to."

Fifteen minutes later they checked out with chicken strips, potato wedges and ranch dressing from the deli, a bag of pretzels, some apples, diet Coke, unsweetened tea, and a few bottles of water. Not exactly great nutrition, but it would do.

Storm drove out of the parking lot. "Eat," she told her father. "While it's still warm."

The sun was sliding through a pink and orange sky, light fading. She turned the radio up, playing an oldies rock station. Her father was studiously eating.

She could tell he'd been hungry by the eager way he attacked the meal.

"You want me to drive so you can eat?" he asked, after he'd finished half the chicken.

"No, I just had dinner, she lied. I bought that for you. Besides, do you even have a license?"

"No, I don't have a license but I still remember how to drive. Isn't it like riding a bike?" He gave her an awkward smile, then set the box of food on the console within her reach, opened a fresh packet of ranch dressing and propped it in one corner of the box.

She managed to dip and eat one strip and one potato wedge. It felt like a small victory, but she wasn't sure why. "Could you open a bottle of water for me?" she asked. They were merging onto the highway, moving into heavy traffic.

He did as she asked, handing the bottle to her carefully, so she didn't have to take her eyes from the road.

"Could you put the food away? I'm done."

She half expected an argument about how little she'd eaten and was relieved when he did as she'd asked without comment. Once on the highway, she moved her old but dependable Volvo sedan into the fast lane and stayed there, keeping a car's length from the car in front of her and passing the traffic on her right. The posted speed was sixty, but she ranged between seventy and eighty, depending on traffic in the fast lane. A ticket would be a minor inconvenience compared to getting there fast. This was not going to be a relaxing drive.

After an hour of complete silence, Storm heard a low rumbling and glancing to her right saw that her father had fallen asleep. His head was tilted back against the headrest, and though asleep he seemed tense, his body stiff, his vein-corded hands clenched against his thighs.

The fact of his slumber put Storm more at ease and she was able to gather her thoughts and begin to analyze why she was doing this. She might as well, there was little else to do. After all, she was going to be stuck in a car for hours with the stranger who was her father.

Tom must think she'd lost her mind. He was probably right. If her mother was in danger, why hadn't she called the police? Maybe she didn't need to. Had her father overreacted to what Jackie said, maybe out of some strange need to take on the role of rescuer? Or was Jackie some paranoid whacko who had everyone wound up for nothing?

As she thought about it more, Storm wondered why she herself had been so ready to run to her mother's aid. Wouldn't the normal thing have been to call the lodge and ask whoever answered, be it her mother or this Jackie woman, what the hell was going on. She knew the answer to that line of inquiry before she'd fully formed it.

She didn't want to call her mother. She wanted to see her, face to face. More than that, she wanted her mother to see her and realize that she needed her daughter's help. It was pathetic, but she had to acknowledge there was a certain appeal to playing her mother's white knight, or more accurately, her avenging angel. After all, that was the role she knew best. Maybe she and her father weren't so unalike.

So, there it was, the sad truth. She'd let her father's anxiety drive her to pack a bag and run out like a thoughtless, defiant teenager. A spoiled brat who didn't care who she left behind, who she hurt, just so long as she got what she wanted. And what was that exactly? A mother who gave a damn? Why? Why care about that now?

But that too was a question she had an answer for. When she married Tom she married into a family. An almost made-for-TV-special family. Their children were lucky. They had a set of loving grandparents, an aunt who adored them, all sorts of cousins. She had married into this circle of family who were there for each other. There for weddings, births and funerals. There with hot soup and garlic butter on toast when you were sick. There with cuttings from the roses and lilacs that had grown on the family farm for a hundred years and maybe most important of all, there with stories and roots and a history they didn't appreciate because it was so much a part of them.

Storm had longed for that sort of connection to something, a place, a people. She thought she had begun to find it with Tom. Thought she was building it with him and the kids. But it always felt like her side of the marriage was a bit thin. As if she'd come into it with a load of debt she could never compensate for. It was the lack of family she felt ashamed of. That was the debt. When she married Tom she'd married into a loving family. All Tom got when he married her was a father-in-law in prison and a mother-in-law he'd never met.

She'd tried to make up for these shortcomings by creating the perfect home. They bought the house planning on kids, so she'd made sure the schools were some of the best. She'd studied hard. Learned things she'd never cared about: furniture styles, color, design. She'd bought every piece of furniture, every rug with great care and precision, working toward an idealized vision. Not only did they have the freshly painted house with the white picket fence covered with climbing red roses, but she was also the wife who always kept the place gleaming, the wife who kept her body firm, the mom who brought the party favors, who baked cupcakes, making sure they were nut free and organic.

She had just signed Lindsey up for dance class. Her plan included making sure her kids had plenty of enrichment opportunities shared with kids who would be their friends, the right kind of friends. Eventually they'd go to college, which would be followed by stellar careers, good marriages, and ultimately children.

It was a hell of a lot of work and just lately that role of perfect wife and mother, not to mention full time probation officer, had been taking a back seat to bringing justice to a well deserving few. To do that without getting caught had taken its own share of planning and execution.

She'd felt the change in focus and priority was necessary however. She imagined having a mother who was a convicted killer was worse than growing up in a messy house.

Plus, she figured few husbands would be loyal enough to hang around once they learned their wife's favorite nighttime activity consisted of bringing dark justice to damaged souls. Forget the cops, she almost laughed out loud at the idea of her straight-laced husband sticking around after learning his wife was a murderous vigilante.

There were so many times she wished she could tell him, wished there was someone to share with. The last person she'd been able to do that with had been Lauren.

Lauren. What a mess working with her last year had been. Her father had been responsible for that too. Did he ever think about the young woman he'd hit with his car? Did he regret the pain he'd caused when he got blind drunk and got behind the wheel? She glanced at his sleeping form, then looked quickly away. This wasn't the time to think about blame or revenge. Plenty of time for that later. Right now, the mission was getting to Crescent City and finding out what the hell was going on with her mother.

Nearly three hours later, Storm took Exit 28 then pulled into a rest area, slowing as she entered the parking lot. The change in speed woke Joe. As she pulled into a parking space he sat up, wiped the back of his hand across his mouth and stared around blinking. He seemed disoriented, but the moment passed quickly.

"Rest stop," he said. "How close are we?"

"We're just outside of Eugene so another four hours or so. I need to use the restroom. I imagine you do too. I see there's a coffee cart. You want any?"

He nodded. "Yeah, that would be nice. Thanks."

He hopped out, surprisingly nimble she thought, and strode toward the nearest of two small cinder brick buildings. She yawned, stretched her arms to the ceiling and heard the joints in her shoulders pop. She got out and stretched again. It felt good to be out of the car, smell the fresh air.

In the restroom, she washed her hands, taking a quick look in the mirror. She ran her fingers through her chestnut hair. It was getting long, about time to get it cut again. She pushed her bangs around, fluffing them up a bit so they didn't fall into her eyes. Gotta at least get these bangs cut, she thought, realizing how odd it was to be thinking of something so mundane in the middle of—of whatever this was.

Leaving the restroom, she walked across the lot to the small shack a veteran's group had set up. She returned to the car with two cups of steaming coffee and a paper bag full of donut holes. After unlocking the car, she put the drinks in the cup holders and slid into her seat. Taking a sip of the bitter but welcome coffee she tried to rein in her growing sense of anxiety. Her father was nowhere to be seen.

It was dark out, but street lights were everywhere and between them and the many cars and trucks it was nearly as bright as day. Where the hell was . . . Then she spotted him, walking briskly from an open grassy area that held a few concrete picnic tables. He reached the car and got in.

"Took our empties and garbage and threw it out, then took a quick jog around. Felt good to move a little."

"Your coffee's in the console. Got some donut holes too. Old fashioned I think," she told him.

"Sounds good." He opened the bag, folded back the top and put the bag between them, where she could easily reach.

His good manners were starting to piss her off. In the restroom, she'd washed her hands, pushing up her sleeves to keep them from getting wet. She'd felt the roughness of damaged skin when she touched her wrist. That spider web of scar tissue which served as a constant reminder of what a great father she had.

"Let's go." She started the car, carefully backed up, then got her speed up quickly in order to merge with the traffic on the highway. He seemed to sense her change of mood and said nothing, just sipped at his coffee and stared out at the passing scene.

An hour of silence went by. It was impossible to sustain her anger. She sighed and fished one of the donut holes out of the bag. There was no need to get emotional. No use being angry at her father. He was nothing to her, nothing but the means to an end. An excuse to see her mother and maybe start to fix what had been broken so many years ago. What was broken between her and her father, well, that was beyond repair.

"Mind if I change the station on the radio?" he asked.

"Go ahead."

As he scanned through the channels, she amused herself by reading the billboards that dotted the highway. First up, a word about a local casino urging people to come and play, followed by a dire warning about teenage pregnancy. After that was a colorful ad for an adult bookstore, followed by a rather grisly ad on the evils of abortion and then another ad for a casino.

It seemed as if everyone was against abortions and pregnancy but all in for pornography and gambling. The messages probably contained some deeper meaning but trying to make sense of it would only give her a headache.

The next billboard, since billboards are usually a means of selling something, appeared to be selling the possibility of forgiveness through Jesus, who apparently hung out at a particularly nice church with stunning stained glass and fantastic architecture. Well, he was a carpenter, after all, she thought, smiling a little at the mild heresy.

"There's a great message," she said, "First we gamble, do a little porn, get knocked up, maybe get an abortion but it's all good, just toss a little money to the church and bang, forgiven."

"So, not much of a church-goer I gather," her father said.

Storm hadn't realized she'd spoken out loud. Too much quiet in this car, she decided. Too much quiet could make you crazy to fill the silence.

"No. Not so much," she agreed.

"Your mom and I, neither one of us was very religious. Guess we passed that on."

"Guess so. I imagine if I did step into a church I'd probably burst into flames." She bit her lip and her hands tightened on the steering wheel. Had she nearly shared too much?

"I know we've never spoken about that night," he said. "I wanted to go to the hospital, but your mother was so angry. Then there was the accident, jail, court, prison. I wanted to write. Tried a few times, but the letters were so . . . They weren't enough."

And here it was, the moment she'd dreaded. Talking about that night.

For the first ten years of her life her father had been gone much of the time. When he did come home it was cause for celebration. She'd loved him so much, missed him so hard. Then he'd had one fist fight too many and the military decided they could get along just fine without him. The long-awaited home coming had been great—for a while. Then the arguments had begun, the harsh words, the new rules that varied depending on the amount and type of alcohol. Those rules were complex, and she never did figure them out.

Days were school and the dread of going home. The growing realization that the dad she'd loved had become an angry drunk she didn't understand. Worse, she was afraid of him, and she hated herself for that fear. She hated the coward who slunk to her bedroom as soon after dinner as she could. The girl who buried herself in books and tried to ignore the angry shouts and slaps and later the sound of tears from the other side of her parent's bedroom door.

"What you did. It was a horrible, horrible thing." Storm could hear her thirteen-year-old-self in those words of accusation.

"I know."

"You don't know shit. You don't know what it's like to have your own father pour his stinking damn liquor on you and then light you on fire. You don't know what it's like to feel your blouse melt into your skin. To smell your hair sizzle. You don't know what it's like when they come for you in the hospital and ask you not to move when they know damn well you can't move, you're strapped down tight. You can't fight. All you can do is scream and scream and pray your mom or your dad will show up and make them stop, or at least hold your fucking hand while they torture you. You son of a bitch."

Storm jerked the steering wheel and drove the car onto the shoulder. Gravel tapped the undercarriage. Someone honked. She pumped the brakes and the car slowed, came to a stop on the edge of a ditch but safely off the highway. The slip stream from the cars racing by buffeted the Volvo so it rocked slightly as if they were far out at sea.

They sat, not speaking for a while, then Storm: "Do you know for a long time I thought Mom was dead. That you had killed her?"

"But—"

"Yeah, I know. She's not dead."

"How could you think I could kill your mother?"

Storm turned in her seat to confront him, this monster who had haunted her nightmares most of her life. In the flashes of light from the passing headlights she saw a man, nothing more, tears following the track of wrinkles that bracketed his mouth.

He said, "I don't get how you could think that. I mean, sure I was a drunk. I could even be a mean drunk, but I never hurt you before that day. I never hurt your mother. No, I'm lying," he said correcting himself. He rubbed his hands across his face. "We'd have fights. I slapped her sometimes. She hit me back too. It wasn't pretty. You must have heard. I never thought how it . . . I'm so sorry. I can't stop saying that.

I know it's not worth much to you. But still, kill your mom? She was my life. That's crazy."

"Really?" she asked, her voice dripping with sarcasm. "That's crazy? A nasty, unpredictable fucking drunk that kept his family on tiptoe like we were walking on eggshells all the time, and you think I was crazy to think you killed Mom? You set me on fire!"

Storm took a deep breath and sat back in her seat, breaking eye contact. "The thing I find ironic is that it was Mom and not me who lost her mind."

"That don't come close to being funny. I know you don't believe me but that night, it destroyed me. It cut me into little pieces."

"Am I supposed to feel sorry for you now?" Storm demanded, turning again to face him. Behind him, she could barely make out the spindly arms of an irrigation system against the darker backdrop of fields, and a moonlit sky.

"Of course not. I'm just . . . I had no idea. I was such a damn mess back then. Drugs and drinking and my head all messed up. I'm not trying to make excuses."

"Good, because there aren't any for the fucked-up shit you did," she spat out scathingly. "You know, the fire, the fire wasn't even the worst of it."

And now Storm felt it, that sense of gathering darkness, that dismal center deep in her stomach. But she was grateful for it. Only that malevolent force gave her courage.

"Do you remember how it started? I was late coming home from a sleep over. You said my friend and I were lesbians. I hardly knew what that word meant, but you made it sound so ugly. I tried to walk past you, get to my room but you didn't like that. You grabbed my arm and pulled me onto your lap. You stank of booze and cigarettes. I was disgusted by you. I was hurt by your accusations.

"You dragged me onto your lap and when I tried to get free you put your hand on me. Remember that? You put your hand on my breast and wouldn't let me go. You said you owned me. Every fucking inch. You could do what you wanted. You acted the part of a pedophile. I was too young to know what that word meant either. Do you remember that, father?" Storm's question, so precise and articulate, so weirdly calm, turned each word into a hammer blow.

He turned away from her, staring out the window or at his own reflection. Storm couldn't tell which.

"I do remember," he said in a harsh whisper. "I remember in my dreams, in my therapy sessions. I remembered it when I was drunk and when I was sober and when I tried to kill myself with jail-house hooch. It was in every one of the letters I tried to write to you, to apologize and to explain. I wanted to tell you it wasn't about sex, it was about anger and power and a need to control one damn thing in my life. I wanted to explain, ask you to forgive me. But how do you say that to a thirteen-year-old kid? Where do you start? I couldn't. I was a coward."

"You got that right," Storm snapped. But her anger, so hot it was homicidal, could not be unleashed. There was a job ahead, and Storm had rules. Four rules that kept her safe: no blood, no bodies, no trophies and no connections.

She would still the sizzling energy that wound through her, for now. Later, she would find time to reconsider the rules and how she might bend them to deal with her father but for now. . .

"Let's go find Mom."

CHAPTER FOUR

THE FADING PULSE OF THE motorcycles brought Storm and her father to their feet.

"Sounds like they're several blocks over and heading back toward the lodge." Joe said.

Storm, her head cocked toward the sound, nodded her agreement. "We can probably get out of here now."

"Sounds good to me."

The walk to the car was uneventful. Nothing moved. The neighborhood of day workers was still, everyone tucked in for the night. Storm drove toward the dim glow of town, stopping at the first motel she saw. The single-story building looked worn out. It was pale yellow with avocado green trim and a flat, red-shake roof. Pots of leggy petunias stood in front of the office. Nothing else disturbed the expanse of broken asphalt that made up the parking lot, except for an old white Chevy pickup and an older gray Ford sedan, both backed in as if their owners might need to make a hasty getaway.

Storm went in and rang the bell. A sleepy man with disheveled hair padded out barefoot to stand behind the counter. He'd come through a door marked "Office" which he left open behind him, affording her a view of a messy living room and a couch made up as a bed.

She paid for two rooms, got two magnetic keys and a well-rehearsed speech about coffee and muffins available at 6 AM. The man was stumbling back toward his bed before she reached the door.

Storm got back in the car, drove down the sloping lot and parked, nose in, in front of number twelve. "You're in eleven," she told her father, handing him a magnetic key.

"We need to make a plan," her father said.

She looked at him, his skin yellow under the dim glow of porch lights. "We need to sleep. We'll plan tomorrow."

He looked like he was forming an argument, but then shrugged and gave in.

Storm lay on the too hard bed, under stiff sheets, and wished Tom were there to snuggle against. Rolling to her side she took the extra pillow and clutched it to her. It was cold and smelled metallic, like the ocean. It was a poor substitute for her husband, who was hundreds of miles away and probably sleeping. What had he been thinking before he drifted off, she wondered. She picked up her phone, charging on the nightstand and sent Tom a text saying she'd arrived in Crescent City and was safe.

Had he been thinking his wife had lost her mind, that she'd finally gone too far? Was he considering the cost of divorce and what kind of custody arrangements were in his future? A single tear slid from her eye, trickled across the bridge of her nose and fell. *Stop it.* With an incredible act of will she forced her thoughts to a different subject.

Tomorrow. What will you do tomorrow? She imagined driving back to the lodge, this time in daylight. Meeting her mother for the first time in years. Finding out why her mother was putting up with bikers, most importantly bad ass bikers, not some friendly group of retired guys with an expensive hobby.

Storm yawned. Tried to think, to plan, but sleep rolled over her like a dark wheel, pushing away all her thoughts.

She woke at six, showered and dressed quickly, then went to the office for coffee. She found her father already there, settled all alone in the hotel's breakfast room, a bowl of cereal and a blueberry muffin in front of him. His hand was curled around a small Styrofoam cup that gave off steam and the heavenly scent of strong coffee. She poured herself a cup, grabbed a cranberry orange muffin from the small stack of plastic-wrapped offerings that lined the short counter, and joined him.

"We could find a better breakfast somewhere," he offered, as she sat down across from him. She shrugged.

"It's fine. What's our plan?"

"Right to it, huh?" Joe said.

"What if it's complete chaos there. That guy I . . ." Her gaze darted around the room. They were alone, but still she didn't finish the sentence.

"I called this morning, talked to Jackie," Joe said. "You didn't hurt him, not much anyway. The bullet sort of breezed by, barely scraped the skin. Jackie said they think it was a hunter who mistook him for a deer."

"Hunting at night? Isn't that illegal."

Joe shrugged. "Would that stop everyone?"

"No, of course not."

"Anyway, you were asking about our plan. I figure we roll up and check in," suggested Joe.

"Just check in?"

"Yes. It's a lodge and that's what people do. They check in."

"You don't think my mother will freak out when she sees us?"

"Jackie agreed to clue your mom in so that she's not surprised. We'll play it from there."

Storm rubbed at a stiff shoulder. She hadn't slept well. The world felt grainy and her father's plan seemed disappointingly simple. "So, we just check in, wait until we're alone with her and ask what the hell is going on?"

"Yeah, basically."

Storm took a sip of coffee and sighed.

"You got a better idea?" Joe asked.

"Sadly, no."

Storm packed the little clothes she had in her carry on and put it in the trunk. "You can put your backpack in that duffel bag in the trunk. It looks more like luggage," she told him. If we're pretending we planned to stay at the lodge, we should at least have luggage. That pack makes you look like you're getting ready to hit the Pacific Crest Trail."

"Good idea. Oh, and while we're talking logistics, I think we should get rooms next to each other or better yet, share one."

"Why?"

"So I can keep an eye out for you. At least until we know who these men are and what they want. Though, after last night, I might be more worried about them than I am about you."

Storm almost smiled. Who, she wondered, would be protecting whom? "You think she'll be happy with the idea of us coming to rescue her?" she asked. "It's her life and her customers. What if she decides to kick us out? Or what if these bikers are harmless and Jackie's nuts?"

"I think you already know the answer to that. The way they came after us last night. How ready, not to mention fast, they were to react. That wasn't the response of harmless men."

"Probably not," Storm grudgingly agreed.

There was nothing more to say.

As they drove up the winding lane they were offered a breathtaking view of the lake on their right. The trees along the distant shoreline and the drifting clouds mirrored on the lake's surface explained its name.

Coming to a straightaway, they saw the lodge on their left. The tall structure, all age darkened wood and glinting windows, sat just off the road at the base of a grassy slope. The slope rose on three sides bounded by trees and gray outcroppings of rock. Looking up past the house Storm recognized the place she and her father had stood the night before, peering down at the lodge. Just beyond the driveway she saw the lawn and the group of white barked trees.

Joe followed her gaze and said, "I'm glad Jackie told me that boy's okay. It's a good thing you're a terrible shot."

"It was downhill, in the dark," Storm reminded him defensively.

"I know. Just teasing."

A smile broke across her face briefly and then, as quickly, disappeared.

"Well, Jackie says they'll be expecting us."

"Good."

Storm pulled into the driveway, which was wide enough to accommodate three rows of three cars. She parked in the lane closest to the front steps, next to a light green Subaru Outback that sat in the center row. On the far side of it was a dark blue Ford pickup with what looked like cages for dogs in the bed. Behind it, two Harley Davidson motorcycles had been backed in. The bikes had custom paint and black leather bags. They were dusty, their leather seats cracked and worn. They looked as if they'd seen a lot of miles. Beyond that they told her nothing.

They got out, took their bags from the trunk and, with Storm taking the lead, climbed the steps to the front porch. The door had a sign that read, 'Welcome Please Come In'. Storm opened the door and a bell jingled to announce their arrival.

As they entered, they were greeted by a slender woman Storm judged to be in her early sixties, with a blond pixie cut and sharp blue eyes. She smiled and said, "Storm. So nice you made it." Looking past Storm to Joe her smile grew even wider. "Come in. Come in," she told them. "I'm Jackie, and I'm glad you called to let me know you were coming. Though of course I'd have recognized Storm right off."

Storm gave the woman a questioning look.

"Oh, you'll see. Anyone who's ever stayed here would recognize you in a heartbeat. Of course your mom calls you Willow about as often as she calls you Storm. Old habit I guess. I like both but I hear you prefer Storm. Is that right?"

Storm wondered if the woman always talked this fast, or if it was because she was nervous.

"Here, let's check you in, then we can talk."

Storm found herself in an entry with high ceilings and wood paneling on the walls. To the right, a wide staircase led to the second floor and a railed landing. To the left an open doorway gave her a glimpse of leather sofas, the edge of an old piano and dark red, oriental carpet. At the back a french door with white lace curtains obscured the view of the back of the house.

A narrow desk stood near the center of the entry. Barely larger than a podium, it held a bowl of flowers and an open registration book. Jackie stood behind the desk while Joe signed them in. Then she pulled out a drawer, removed two keys and handed one to each of them.

"We only have one room left. You'll have to share. There's a queen-sized bed and a roll out cot in the closet you can set up. It's the first room at the top of the stairs. It's named the Meadowlark. There's a nameplate on the door so you won't have any trouble finding it." She looked toward the french door and Storm thought her voice rose in volume. "Muffins, scones and fresh coffee are available at seven in the morning. Lunch is served at noon but if you're late there's always something in the kitchen until about two. Dinner is at six. Here's a brochure with things to do in the area. You'll find more information about those in your room."

Joe leaned toward Jackie and Storm heard his urgent whisper. "Where's Lisa?"

"Oh, I'm sorry, didn't I tell you. She's gone on a ride with one of our guests. A ride on a motorcycle. Doesn't that sound nice?"

Storm didn't think so but said nothing.

"When do you think she'll be back?" Joe asked.

A line in Jackie's forehead deepened and she shrugged. "No idea," she replied.

"Where are the rest of them?" he asked.

She looked toward the french door again. "On the back deck," she whispered. "That's where they spend most of their time. She won't let them smoke inside."

"That's good." Then, resuming his normal tone he said, "Thanks, we'll go put our things away."

"Wonderful. Then when you come back I can give you both a tour."

"That would be nice," said Joe.

The rapid talking and the stilted conversation made Storm feel uncomfortable, even vulnerable. Jackie seemed jumpy, maybe even panicky. It was an emotion she knew could be contagious, and dangerous. Besides, she was already tired of playing this game. She wanted to take action.

"She knows you're coming," Lisa said quietly. "She's not happy. Maybe this was a mistake. I told you about the trouble last night. One of the men getting shot."

"You said it was a hunter," her father said.

"Well, we thought so at the time. It was really late. After midnight or just around then. I was up though, sitting in bed reading. I heard he went outside to feed their dogs and someone shot at him. Didn't do much, just grazed his neck. They bandaged him up okay. Lisa was the one who thought it must have been a hunter trying for a deer but me, I don't know. You read a lot about gangs, drive by shootings. The whole thing makes me anxious. I wish they'd just leave."

"Well, we'll have to see what we can do to make that happen," said Joe.

"Good."

Standing on the landing, looking down over the waist-high rail, gave Storm a slightly dizzying view of the entryway. She looked away, turning her attention to the second floor.

There were eight doors off the landing. Six held brass plates with the names of birds, two were marked with the universal symbols for bathroom. All the doors were periwinkle blue, the walls a rather dull yellow. Both were scuffed and in need of fresh paint.

They entered Meadowlark, and Storm shut the door behind them and took a quick look around. The room was pretty much as she'd imagined. The wall to her right held a narrow window with blinds and white curtains with a pattern of green leaves. They were tied back and the blinds were up giving her a good view of the side yard and what she'd begun to think of as the dog's area.

Two white wicker chairs on either side of the window provided seating. Slightly off center and against the far wall, the queen-bed, with a metal headboard painted white but distressed to look old, was covered with a colorful quilt and at least a dozen pillows. To either side, small dressers served the dual purpose of providing storage for clothing and a surface for lamps, a small television, and an alarm clock. A door on the left opened to reveal a shallow closet that held only a row of plastic hangers and the roll-up cot Jackie had mentioned. The room was small but cozy, the kind of place Storm would have loved to take Tom for a weekend getaway.

For a moment she let herself imagine them sitting in the dining room at breakfast. Tom would make the other guests laugh and she'd sit quietly beside him and soak up the ambiance she had no part of creating. She wondered where he was, what he was doing, why he hadn't called or texted her back. No, she knew why. He was angry, and he had every right to be.

Joe dropped the duffel bag on the floor and took one of the chairs. It creaked a protest to his weight.

"Never liked this wicker stuff," he said, shifting his weight and earning another squeal.

"Me either," she agreed. "But the rest of the room's okay. At least it's not pink."

"Thank heaven for small favors."

She nodded, took a seat on the edge of the bed, then asked, "Downstairs, when we were checking in, why did you say it was good that the men were on the deck. Do you have a plan?"

Joe paused a moment, as if trying to remember, then said, "No, I didn't mean the location was good, I meant making them smoke outside was good. It means they aren't in total control. It means your mother has some sway over them."

"Oh, I see. That's an interesting insight."

"It doesn't mean your mother's not in trouble."

"No, but it might. Maybe Jackie got it all wrong."

"Maybe, but I still don't take her as someone who would make up stories or exaggerate things," said Joe.

"So, what now?" asked Storm.

"Now I guess we wait for your mother to get back from wherever she's gone and then we find a way to get her aside for a serious talk."

Storm nodded, then said, "Can you see Mom on the back of a motorcycle? I mean, how old is she, fifty-five or more?"

"That's not old. Besides, your mom was something of a wild child in her day. It's not that out of the question. Hell, we used to own a couple dirt bikes and she rode plenty."

Storm couldn't imagine it. She'd constructed an image of her mother based on the memories of a thirteen-year-old. When she tried hard she could remember her face. Her brown hair worn in a long braid, Dark brown eyes full of warmth. A ready laugh. She remembered a woman who was in the kitchen a lot, with steam hovering around her, a wooden spoon in hand. A woman with yellow gloves and pink garden shoes digging in the garden. The memories were snippets, fractured images that somehow combined became the person she had called Mom.

Nowhere in that was there a memory of a woman on a motorcycle. Were her memories even real or were they some constructed mixture of made-for-television mothers? She supposed, in a little while, she'd have an answer to that.

CHAPTER FIVE

AS A PROBATION OFFICER, Storm had faced her share of angry, even violent clients. As a vigilante she'd dealt with cruel, abusive psychopaths without a shred of compassion. She'd been afraid of some of them, of their capacity for cruelty, and eventually of her own. But nothing she had seen or done had made her hands shake the way they did as she awaited the arrival of her mother. She wrung them together, unconsciously mimicking her father's nervous habit.

The popcorn popper burble of a Harley engine grew. She was back. Joe had gone in search of a restroom. Should she wait for him? Go look for him? She stepped out of the bedroom onto the landing and was surprised at the amount of relief she felt at seeing him walking toward her. He joined her at the top of the stairs and when they shared a glance she realized he was as nervous as she was. Mentally steeling herself, she looked down into the entryway as the door swung open and two people, a man and a woman, came in.

The man was broad-shouldered, with short brown hair, a beard, but she barely saw him. Most of her attention was on the woman. She was short and slender with gray hair tied in a messy bun. She wore a soft pink, button-down shirt with a shirttail hem that hung over a pair of crisply ironed jeans and white sneakers. Storm devoured every detail. Then the woman looked up to say something to the man and saw Storm.

Both women stood, their eyes locked on each other's.

The moment held until Joe broke it by saying, "Lisa."

"Joe." Storm's mother said, her eyes darting from one to the other. "Storm." Her voice was a breathless whisper.

Then with visible effort she turned to the man she'd come in with, who had also turned to look up at them, and said, "Leon, this is my daughter, Storm, and my ex-husband, Joe." From the calm tone of her mother's voice, Storm didn't get the sense that anything was wrong between them. On the other hand, the appearance of her and Joe hadn't seemed to phase her either. Maybe she was just a really good actor.

"Something you planned?" Leon asked pleasantly enough.

"No," said Lisa, "but family, you know how they are, they drop by whenever they want."

"Of course. Well, don't let me get in the way. We'll talk later." He nodded to Joe and Storm then walked toward the door at the back of the entry with the easy confidence of familiarity.

The two of them walked down the stairs until they reached the first floor. Then, the three of them stood and faced each other. In the few moments of strained silence Storm was sure she could hear her heart beating.

"I don't . . . I'm not sure what . . ." Storm's mother stumbled to express herself, for the first time revealing emotion. "I've wanted to see you for so long. I can't believe how beautiful you are. I've been..."

Storm watched her mother put the palms of her hands against her face, almost as if she were playing a child's game of peek-a-boo or trying to hide.

Finally she lowered them, turned her attention to Joe. "I heard you'd been released," she said, "but I didn't think you'd come looking for me. Let alone with our daughter. Why are you both here? Together? Why would you— Oh wait, I get it, Jackie's involved in this, isn't she? How did she find you? What did she tell you?"

"Let's find someplace we can sit and talk, what do you say? And maybe some coffee?" Joe suggested.

"Of course. Yes, of course." Lisa looked around the entryway blankly. She was obviously overwhelmed and relieved to have something to do. "Let's go to the kitchen. There's a breakfast nook and plenty of coffee, or tea if you prefer. Have you had breakfast?" Storm saw calm partially restored as her mother slipped into the familiar role of host.

The kitchen was large, with wood cabinets and butcher block countertops. A white granite topped island held a commercial-sized coffee urn, an electric kettle and a tray of white ceramic coffee mugs.

"What would you like, coffee, tea?"

"Coffee," Storm and her father said simultaneously.

"Cream and sugar is in the basket next to the coffee pot. Help yourselves," said Lisa, as she poured them each a cup.

Lisa and Joe carried their black coffees to a nook that held a round table and four chairs.

Storm took her cup and busied herself adding cream and sugar from the basket. She kept her back to her parents, her hands were still shaking and when she tried to tear a packet of sugar open it ripped in half, spreading sugar across the otherwise pristine surface. She swept it up with the edge of her hand, found a garbage can at one end of the island and threw it in, rubbing her hands together to get rid of the sticky grains. By the time she joined them she felt calm enough to not spill her coffee. She was even fairly sure she could speak without her voice cracking and giving away her anxiety. Maybe Jackie wasn't the only nervous one, she decided.

Taking a seat next to her father, and across from her mother she couldn't help but study the woman. She noticed her mother's hair was several shades of gray, from a sort of dirty nickel to cotton ball white. Soft strands had come free from the bun and framed and softened her look. She saw that her mother's face was the same shape as her own, a long oval. Her features were also similar, brown eyes, slightly arched brows, a nose that was a little too long, lips a little too thin. It was an average face, Storm thought, enriched with a tracing of laugh lines around the mouth and a smattering of crow's feet at the corner of the eyes.

". . . but they aren't a problem," Storm heard her mother say as she tuned back into their conversation. "In fact, one of them gave me a ride around the lake this morning, just for fun."

"Just for fun? You looked white as a ghost when you walked in that door," said Joe.

"Maybe that was because of you."

"Bullshit, you hadn't even seen us yet."

"Nothing changes, does it, twenty years and you're still calling bullshit on me." She shook her head then picked up her mug and sipped her coffee, clearly not intimidated. "I did get a little motion sick on the bike. Getting a little too old for that kind of thing," she said with a self-deprecating shrug.

Storm realized that though they hadn't seen each other in a long time there was a history there. A familiarity with each other, even a comfortable sort of banter, all the while she'd been expecting guns at twenty paces.

She picked up her own coffee, took a tentative sip, looked across the table and noticed that she and her mother held their cups the same way, cradled in two hands. Inside, deep in that well where Storm kept her emotions safely at bay, something stirred. Something rose up, sharp as dragon's teeth or cat's claws, a bright and keening pain that brought with it the prospect of tears. She swallowed it down. This was not the time.

"I'm glad you're here," Lisa said, looking at Storm, and tears did appear in *her* eyes. "I've wanted to see you for so long." She knuckled the tears away, then looked down at the table, staring hard at the scarred wood surface. "But I knew I didn't deserve having you in my life. I figured, if you wanted to see me you'd let me know. If you didn't, well, that was my price to pay, my sentence, you know?" She looked up and her eyes swept them both.

Joe shook his head. "I get how you feel that way, but you can't blame yourself for having a breakdown. You were not well, and I put you there. It's on me, all of it. You need to let it go. Both of you do," he said looking into Storm's eyes. "This is a chance for a new beginning, a new future, for the two of you."

"Maybe," said Storm, "but first we need to deal with whatever's going on here and now."

"Nothing. Nothing is going on," said Lisa. "Just like I was telling your father." Lisa sat back in her chair, her lips pursed. "Jackie called you," she said to Joe. "I suspected the two of you had talked. You shouldn't put too much stock in what Jackie says. She's been a lot of help and I consider her a friend, but she's also a drunk and not always to be trusted."

"A drunk?" asked Storm.

"Yes. She's a binge drinker. She'll be fine for weeks, even months, then something will set her off. She'll find a cheap hotel with a bar and drink herself blind until closing. She'll stay there until she's good and ready, then get a friendly bartender to call me for a ride. I know it's strange, but she's too ashamed to call me directly. I'll pick her up, bring her home, and in a few days she's usually okay. Of course, sometimes she's not okay, and the withdrawal is so bad I end up taking her to the hospital. Once it's over she's fine until the next time and there's always a next time."

"You're saying we can't believe her?" said Storm.

"I'm saying it depends on what day it is," said Lisa. "All those years of drinking have affected her. She gets paranoid sometimes. I'm betting this is one of those times."

"So, these bikers aren't forcing you to let them stay here?" asked Joe.

Lisa's eyes went wide. "Why, heck no. How would they do that? Why? That's the silliest thing I've heard all year. I mean, sure, they look a little rough and their language might not be up to some folk's standards, but they pay and, if you look around, you'll notice we could use some money around here."

"Well, that's a relief, not the needing money part, but the part where I thought they were taking advantage of you in some way," said Joe. "Jackie told us she was worried they were up to something, maybe something criminal. That they acted sketchy enough that she thought normally you'd kick them out, but they won't let you."

"Won't let me? In my own place?"

Lisa's shock seemed real, thought Storm. But there was something just a little off, like a song you know well, played in a different key.

"You should know better, Joseph Dean. Did you drag my Willow, I mean Storm, away from her family for such a silly thing? Sorry," she said to Storm. "Your aunt told me you changed your name and I try to remember but . . ." She spread out her arms in a gesture meant to convey how hopeless the attempt was.

Storm had cringed at the use of the name her mother had given her. "Willows are amazing," she'd told Storm when she was little, "They bend but never break before a storm." But Storm hadn't wanted to bend, she'd wanted to *be* the storm, so she'd had her name legally changed as soon as she turned eighteen. No one had called her Willow for a long time.

"I guess I did sort of drag her here," said Joe. "Though she did the driving. I'm glad we came, because at least it gives you two a chance to talk."

"Is that something you want?" Lisa asked, leaning forward, her dark eyes locked on Storm's. Anxiety written on every line of her face.

"I . . . I think so." Storm managed. She'd always wanted that. Had always wanted her mother in her life, but now that she had the chance, she struggled with admitting it. She'd barely arrived, and it felt like things were going so quickly and this woman, whose more youthful face she saw in flashes of memory, this woman was virtually a stranger.

"I'm so glad," Lisa said, and she reached across the table and put the tips of her fingers on Storm's forearm. The touch was like an electrical connection, crackling with suppressed power, and emotion.

Just then the same man that had ridden in with Lisa walked into the kitchen. Storm struggled to remember his name. Leo?

"Time for a refill," he said, giving them a friendly smile and reaching for the coffee pot.

Storm noticed details she hadn't seen at first. There was a line drawing of a winged skull on the front of his t-shirt. There was a tattoo, some sort of tribal design around each bicep. He was well groomed, his beard neatly trimmed, his light brown hair almost as militarily short as her father's. He had regular features, and Storm thought most women would find him attractive. He was a little taller than average, maybe six feet, and his body looked strong, tight, as if he worked out regularly, or had been blessed with good genetics.

The two times Storm had heard him speak he'd been friendly and polite. Nothing about him seemed particularly sinister or rang alarm bells, but she knew that meant little. More than once one of her clients had surprised her by pairing an ordinary appearance with extraordinary actions.

Once he'd filled his cup he raised it to them in a mock salute then strode out of the kitchen. As soon as he left the conversation resumed.

"I'd sure like to know what the whole deal is with him and the rest of them," said Joe. "You say they're just guests, but they sure rattled Jackie, and from what you've said about her she's no saint. If she hangs out at bars regularly she's had to have seen some pretty rough characters. Why would these ones worry her so much?"

"I already told you. You and Jackie are inventing problems where there are none." Lisa stared hard at Joe, as if maintaining direct eye contact would convince him she was telling the truth. At the same time, she unconsciously reached up and brushed the side of her nose and cheek with her fingers.

Storm recognized the gesture as one associated with lying. Body Language 101 had been one of the more interesting classes she'd taken as preparation for her job as a probation officer.

"I'm being a terrible host," Lisa said, changing the subject. "Have the two of you eaten? We keep scones in the fridge or I could whip up some bacon and eggs?"

"We ate at the motel," said Joe.

"I'm good," agreed Storm. "Where's Jackie?" She wanted to get the other woman aside and talk to her. As much as she wanted to believe her mother, she'd still like to know what Jackie had seen or heard to convince her that they were forcing Lisa to host them.

"Haven't seen her since I got back. Probably dusting something, or out in the garden. It's a nice day and she never stops moving."

"A good trait in an employee," said Joe. "Probably makes up for the other stuff."

"It does," agreed Lisa.

Storm found the conversation both fascinating and boring. She hadn't imagined what she'd be dealing with, but none of her imaginings had included small talk.

"I'd like to see your garden," she said, thinking if that was where Jackie was, it would be a good place to be.

"Of course," said Lisa, getting up so eagerly she bumped the table, spilling some of Storm's barely touched coffee. Storm grabbed a crocheted washcloth that was hanging near the sink and wiped up the spill. Lisa gathered their cups and the two women awkwardly bumped into each other. Storm turned back to the sink, rinsing and re-rinsing the cloth.

She'd wanted to see her mother for a long time, but the timing was terrible. She should be home, with Tom, Lindsey and Joel. She should be with her family, not with these strangers. If her mother wasn't in danger, then there was no good reason for taking off so suddenly, leaving Tom to deal with everything. Well, she would be going home soon. She'd see the garden, have a quick chat with Jackie, make plans to visit her mother at a better time, and then she'd get out of here. There was only one nagging problem.

The dog.

The view from Meadowlark's window included the group of white barked trees where the dogs were chained. Each time Storm thought of the poor, terrified dog, curled in a fetal position in a failed attempt to protect itself, it made her feel sick. She couldn't leave without that dog.

"The garden's right off the back deck," Lisa was saying brightly. "Makes it easier to haul things in for the kitchen. Jackie's got a bunch of herbs potted back there. She drags them onto the deck when the weather gets cold. Not that it ever gets that cold, of course. But still, we do get the occasional hard freeze."

Storm followed her parents out of the kitchen and into the huge open room that served as both a dining and living area. Toward the rear of the house, arranged along a wall of windows, were three rectangular wood tables and a variety of mismatched chairs. Toward the front of the house, the living area held a rock fireplace, gleaming pine walls, overstuffed leather furniture and an old piano. Decorative touches included baskets of sugar pine cones and carved wood bears. It was rustic and inviting. Near the fireplace, a built-in bookcase formed a cozy niche. A recliner and reading lamp had been arranged in the space. The bookcase held dozens of selections, and lots of framed photographs hung close together.

Immediately drawn to look at the pictures, Storm crossed the room, then froze, her mouth dropping open. Most of the photos were of her. Her as a child on a bike, at the front of a class she didn't remember, her with a gap-toothed smile receiving some sort of award with a ribbon. Her high school graduation, with Aunt June's arm around her shoulders.

Then there were the family shots. Her with Tom and both the kids in the yard of their home. The familiar white picket fence and red roses were unmistakable. She even remembered the day. They'd bought a funny, squiggly thing you attached to the end of a hose. It jumped around sending streams of water randomly. The kids had loved it, running to escape the water creature, laughing like maniacs. There were also shots of the kids, sometimes one, sometimes both, at the playground, playing hopscotch in the driveway, Lindsey, in last year's Christmas play. But who had taken the picture? She turned to Lisa. "Where did you get these? How did you—?"

"I'm still your mother," she said softly. "Their grandmother. Even though I wasn't there I wanted to know how you were. Aunt June sent me pictures. Sometimes, if there was a public event, she'd let me know and if I could manage it I'd show up, hide in the audience."

"But you never told me you were there." Storm said, not sure how she felt about this. Was she angry? Sad? Happy? She needed time to think.

Lisa shrugged. "You were better off without me. At least, that's what I thought. I know you'll never forgive me. I was never the parent that you are. I've seen you with your kids. You take my breath away. They're so amazing. I didn't know what it would feel like to be a grandparent." She held up her hand, palm toward Storm as if to forestall what she might say so she could say it first.

"Yes, I know, I haven't been a grandparent. I've never even met your children, but for some reason I still feel a connection to them, a love for them that was a huge surprise to me. I'd like to meet them someday. They wouldn't have to know who I am. I'd just like to . . . oh it doesn't matter." She rubbed her arms as if they were cold. "Let's go find Jackie so she can tell you she was mistaken, and you can get out of here and get back home to them."

CHAPTER SIX

Storm spotted an embroidered patch that read "1%" on one of the sleeves. She didn't know a lot about motorcycle clubs, but she'd once read that some motorcycle organization had stated that ninety-nine percent of motorcyclists were law-abiding citizens, which meant at least one percent were outlaws.

To openly wear a such a patch seemed like a truly stupid thing to do, thought Storm. Sort of an advertisement asking the police to pay attention to you. But then most of the criminals she'd met in her career hadn't exactly been geniuses.

As they neared the table Storm felt her father tense. She wanted to caution him to stay calm, but the best she could do was put her hand on his shoulder. He glanced at it, gave her a brief smile that said he got the message.

Lisa said, "Let me formally introduce all of you. You've met, Leon."

Leon, not Leo Storm corrected herself, recognizing the man who'd come in with her mother. He gave them a ready smile and she noticed even white teeth a movie star would envy. He wore a tight black t-shirt, torn blue jeans and lace up leather boots.

"This is Martin," she said, and nodded to the man sitting across from Leon.

Martin stood, reached to shake their hands, first Joe's then hers. Taking her hand from her father's shoulder she reached out to shake. Martin's hand was warm, his grip firm. She noticed that he, like Leon, had wide shoulders, narrow hips, and was around six feet tall. His skin was darker than Leon's, Latino maybe Storm thought. He was a good-looking man, with strong features. His dark hair was a little long, a little messy but he was clean shaven. He wore a gray t-shirt, tight around his biceps, washed out jeans and black, square-toed boots.

"I'm sorry, I don't know how to pronounce your name," Storm's mother said to the third man.

"Perro," he said, rolling the r's and dropping his chin in a strange little bob. He was darker than Martin with a narrow face, and a bedraggled beard too thin to hide a weak chin. He was almost skeletally thin. He was dressed all in black, black boots, jeans and shirt, the white tape of a bandage peeking out at the neck.

"And this is Bud," Lisa said, completing the introductions.

Bud was an older white man with a thin moustache and a thick white beard, except around his lips where it was stained yellow. He wore a white t-shirt, with the word Sturgis air brushed across the front, tucked into worn jeans. His boots looked like military issue, laced and cracked with age.

Bud waved a half-full bottle of beer in a gesture of greeting. On the table in front of them sat a shared ashtray half-filled with cigarette butts. The rest of the table was littered with empty cans, bottles, cards and cash.

Storm thought that the way they sat, with their sun-burnt faces close together, their voices low, the sidelong glances, that even without the matching jackets she'd have guessed they belonged to some sort of brotherhood of secrets and conspiracies.

"Nice to meet you Storm said. Hope you're enjoying your stay."

"We are," said Leon. "Your mom's got a nice place. Nice, right Martin?"

"What?" said Martin, stumbling as if it had been a hard question, or as if he were unsure what answer Leon wanted. Then he said, "Yeah, oh sure, real nice."

Storm had no doubt that Leon set the agenda for this particular group.

"Thanks," she said, then took a quick glance at her surroundings.

She stood with her back to the house. Directly ahead was the rugged hillside, topped with the trees and rocks, she and her father had hidden behind the night before. To her right the lawn sloped down to the trees where the dogs were tied. To her left a set of wide steps led off the deck to a well-kept garden. Pots of herbs dotted a narrow, packed gravel path that divided the garden into sections. At one of these sections Jackie was kneeling, loosening the soil with gloved hands.

"Going to give them a tour of the garden and then go for a walk," Lisa explained to the men. A little too much explaining thought Storm, but she gave the men a vacant smile before falling in line behind her mother and father.

"What are you working on?" her mother asked Jackie.

"Cleaning up the weeds around the rosemary. Need any for dinner?"

"Sure, we'll rotisserie a chicken. Lemon rosemary sound good?" she asked, turning to include the men on the deck.

"It does," said Joe. Storm nodded her agreement. Leon raised his beer as a sign of approval.

"Well, you can gather the rosemary later," Lisa said to Jackie. "I thought we'd take a walk, show them around. Why don't you go with us?"

"Sure," agreed Jackie quickly. "I'll just leave these here." She took off her gloves and set them on the edge of the pot.

"Hey!"

Lisa turned in response to the call, shielded her eyes against the sun that was poking from behind the clouds and said, "Yes?"

It was Leon.

"Are you going to be gone long? We need to talk about that friend of mine."

"No, not long, just going up to the viewpoint. We'll be right back."

"Okay. Just checking," he said, and sat back in his chair, sprawled out and easy as if he had not a care in the world.

They followed Lisa, who took a narrow but well worn path and soon Storm found they were crossing through an old apple orchard. The damp had turned the limbs of the trees smoky green with moss and lichen.

"Have to keep an eye out for bears," Lisa warned. "They love the apples but don't show up much until Fall. I'm taking you to a spot just past the orchard that has a fabulous view of the lake. It's my favorite spot. Really quiet and secluded." She didn't say it, but Storm knew she meant a good place to talk privately.

Once beyond the orchard the path wound up and around a hill with small clumps of brush and young pine and fir trees.

"There was a fire here about fifteen years ago," Lisa explained. Everything growing here is pretty young. Soon they lost sight of the lodge. As they reached the top of the hill an open field of grass and wildflowers greeted them. Against the backdrop of a group of boulders thrust from the ground someone had placed two wood benches and a concrete statue of St. Francis.

They all sat down, Storm and her mother taking one bench, Jackie and Joe another, and stared out at the lake as if mesmerized. The rising sun reflecting on its surface sparkled like bright stars across the dark water. The mirror image of the trees along the far shore rippled as a paddler far out on the lake drove his oars into the water. Storm could smell dust and pine and the slightly metallic tang of the nearby ocean. The sun was warm on her face and legs. She leaned back allowing herself, momentarily, to fall under the spell of the place.

After giving them a few minutes to relax, Lisa said, "I know you both want to talk to Jackie about her concerns. Jackie, would you please tell Joe and Storm that you've realized you were wrong?"

Jackie had been stooped forward, her thin elbows resting on her thighs, now she sat up and scrubbed her fingers through her short hair. She sighed, and addressing Joe, who she seemed more at ease with, said rapidly, "Lisa told me that if I didn't tell you the guys were fine and I'm just some paranoid drunk she'd fire me." She shot a defiant glance at Lisa then back to Joe. "I'm not going to do that. I'm not going to lie to save my job. I'd much rather save her ass. Those guys are bad news. I don't know what they want but I'm pretty sure it has to do with drugs. That's what they do, right, these bike gangs? They transport drugs and I don't want any part of it. I don't think Lisa does either. Do you?" she demanded.

"Damn it, what is wrong with you. Don't you have any loyalty?" Lisa's tone was at odds with her words. She sounded pleased, Storm thought. Maybe even relieved that Jackie had refused to lie for her. Storm realized she was pleased too, maybe finally, they'd get to hear the truth.

"Why don't you tell us exactly what's going on here," said Joe.

"Where do I start?" said Lisa.

"How about at the beginning," suggested Joe.

"Fine. Lisa scratched at a dot of pitch on the arm of the bench, keeping her eyes down as she spoke. "About a month ago those men showed up at the door. They asked for a tour and I showed them around."

"Where was I?" Jackie asked.

"You were . . . unavailable," Lisa replied. They all realized this was code for out drinking and said nothing further. Jackie nodded and found something of interest on the lake to stare at.

"After I gave them the nickel tour," continued Lisa, they told me they had a friend at the prison. Pelican Bay is close," she explained. "We get people staying here because they're visiting someone there all the time. Hell, it's probably half our business. The hotels and motels in town even give discounts to those folks. Anyway, they said they wanted to rent all the rooms for a week, and that they'd want to rent a room once a month on a regular basis. The only thing was they couldn't give an exact date. It seemed a little strange to me and I couldn't just hold a room all the time. That's when they told me they wouldn't always need a room. Most of the time what they needed was a safe place to leave a package. They said that someone else might come by and get the package, also about once a month. It was no big deal, just like being a post office and if I was willing to provide that service they'd pay as if they were renting rooms."

"Jesus, that does sound like drugs," Joe said to Jackie.

"What else could it be?" she replied.

"Why would you even consider such a thing?" asked Joe.

Lisa crossed her arms. "Why would I consider such a thing? Have you looked around the place? I mean, yes, I was damn lucky that Mr. Fox left it to me. I was shocked as anyone to realize he'd died with no family and that he thought that much of me. It's a wonderful place, but it's not cheap to maintain. It's got plumbing issues and a roof that's been patched too often and needs a total tear off and replacement. The cedar siding needs to be sealed and the inside needs paint. If it wasn't for Jackie working on the cheap I'd be trying to do it all by myself, and I'd be failing."

Lisa's litany of woes slowly ran down but her arms remained crossed in defiance. "You tell me what you'd do," she asked Joe. "You got some bright ideas to share"

"I could stay. Help out. I used to be pretty good with a hammer. I could delay my plans a little while." His tranquil demeanor, the offer of help, so calmly delivered in response to Lisa's angry tirade took Storm by surprise. "I'm going to Mexico," he explained, He took a deep breath, tilted his face to the sky, as if it were easier to address the clouds than them.

"When I went to prison I was a mess, full of self-pity and pissed at the world. After about ten years of this nonsense, because I'm a slow learner, I finally realized the only one I should be feeling sorry for was you, and Storm, and that young woman I hit with my car when I was so blind drunk I . . . Anyway, that's when I got mad at myself, but that didn't work out so well either. I did stupid things, self-destructive things that caused me to spend another ten years in prison." He looked at Lisa. "Partly, I think I was punishing myself, but also by then I didn't know if I could live a normal life on the outside. I was afraid to leave so I did things to make sure I wouldn't."

"That's awful," said Jackie. "I hate prison. It doesn't help people, just makes them worse."

"I'm not disagreeing with you," said Joe, "but it was probably the best thing for me at the time."

"But times changed?" suggested Lisa.

Joe nodded, "About four years ago I met someone, an older man, a priest, if you can believe that." He gestured toward the statue of St. Francis, the patron saint of animals and nature. The depiction of St. Francis held a dove and an armful of flowers while at his feet a fawn looked up at him adoringly. "He sort of took me on as a pet project, talked to me, counseled me. I admired him. There weren't a lot of people to look up to in that place."

"But he was a prisoner," said Storm. "A criminal."

"Yeah, a real monster. He got caught bringing a truck loaded with illegal immigrants from Central America. They were all young women, girls really, all escaping horrific lives as unwilling prostitutes. They had shared their stories with him and he decided to get them to the states. He had a friend who had a farm in Oregon, in Clackamas County, not far from where you live," Joe said, with a nod to Storm. "He got three years."

"What happened to the girls?" asked Jackie.

"They got sent back home."

"That's awful," said Jackie. "Those poor women."

Joe nodded. "Yeah, it made Father Anthony sad. We used to worry about him. He'd get so depressed. We all knew the minute he got out he'd go right back and try to help them, and he did. He started writing to some of us after he got out. He convinced the church to assign him to work with the people in Michoacán.

He's working with kids who escaped human traffickers or worked for drug cartels. Some of them survived being shot or stabbed so they provide physical therapy, wheelchairs. The work they do there, it's unbelievable. Before Father Anthony I didn't know so many kids were victimized every single day."

"But you can't move to Mexico," said Storm. "You're a felon."

Everyone paused a beat, except for Joe who gave her a wry smile. "Oh, I'll probably find a way to break in."

"He sounds like an amazing person, this priest," said Lisa.

"He is. He taught me, and others at the prison, even some of the guards, what it was to be your best self. You know, before going to prison I never wasted a thought on helping other people but now," he shrugged. "I know it's strange—"

"Strange?" said Storm. "You know this isn't a new story. I've heard it before. Go to jail. Find God. It should be a bumper sticker."

Joe chuckled. "No, not God. I've never been a believer. I've wanted to be, but no, I've never been able to take that leap of faith. For me it's just about doing something good for a change. Call it redemption if you want. Prison is supposed to punish us, make us pay for our sins, but that's a crock. The only way we can pay for sins against man is to help man. That's a direct quote from Father Anthony of course. What about you Storm, do you believe in God?"

Storm stared at the lake, the lone paddler had been joined by two others. They were black lines against the brilliant sparkle of the sun reflecting on the water. A cool breeze stirred the tops of the trees and bent the grass in the meadow, which made a rustling sound, a low hush that was soothing. She said, "I never gave it much thought until the kids were born. Tom has faith and belongs to a church. He takes the kids now and then. We want them to have the experience of going to church and considering faith and religion and God, but we're going to leave it to them to decide. I struggle with it. It would be nice if there was a life after this one, where you would meet up with everyone you cared about." Storm shrugged, "I just don't know. Guess that makes me an agnostic."

They sat in silence, contemplating their own thoughts. Storm shut her eyes for a moment, felt the sun, the cool breeze, let herself concentrate on that and the sound of the grass and nothing more.

Finally, Joe said, "We have to talk about what's going on here, Lisa. We have to put a stop to it. You can't let those men use your home as part of their drug transportation system."

"And you don't have the right to tell me what I can and cannot do," Lisa replied. "I'm glad you and Storm came. I hope we can build something out of this. I want to have a relationship with my daughter. I want to meet my grandchildren. I guess I wouldn't even mind us being friends, but Joe, this isn't the time. You have to go. Both of you have to go."

Joe began to argue but Storm cut him off. "We are going. We won't stay where we're not needed."

She was leaving. However, she wasn't going to go without that poor dog. Unconsciously she tapped her fingers against her chest. Before leaving home, she'd transferred her gun to the new bra holster a coworker had given her. A going away present after she announced she was quitting. She was glad she'd packed it. It was the perfect choice for this situation. Completely hidden and unlikely to be found, even in a pat down. To hell with the fact that it was giving her a heat rash.

"I do want to see you, and Tom and the kids, it's just the timing, that's all," said Lisa.

"Yeah, I get it. Look, I don't like what you're doing. I think it's wrong but if it's what you need to do to survive it's really none of my business. You're an adult. You make your own decisions and you'll suffer the consequences of those decisions. I'm going home. Joe, are you coming with me or are you staying?

"Don't leave yet," said Joe, twisting to look into Storm's eyes. "You should spend some time with your mother."

"Okay, you're staying then," she said and stood up.

CHAPTER SEVEN

HER FATHER FOLLOWED HER, gestured at the others to wait. He caught up to her in the orchard.

"Perro is Spanish for dog," Joe called to Storm's retreating figure.

She turned around, "What?"

"Perro, the guy you shot, the one who was messing with the dogs, they call him dog. Maybe he's not entirely to blame for his behavior."

"Are you kidding me?" Storm asked, "You're making excuses for him? You, of all people?"

"People can change. Maybe no one told him that. But this isn't about him. It's about you. Don't do this," said Joe. "Don't leave. I know you're upset."

Storm stared at her father. "Not upset," she finally said. "Maybe a little disappointed. I think I built my mother up to be someone else in my head. Someone who finally got their life together. I didn't expect her to be someone who would look the other way to make a quick buck."

"Maybe she isn't," said Joe sharply.

Storm dragged her fingers through her hair in frustration, "Now what are you going to tell me?"

"Your mother, the woman I knew, wouldn't look the other way, do nothing. Not without a damn good reason. I don't think people change that much, not even after twenty years. You probably don't remember, but your mother was quite the warrior for justice in her day. She'd never let someone move drugs through her business for money. The only reason I can think of that she'd sit by and do nothing is because she's doing it for someone else, to protect someone. We need to confront her with that. Come back with me. Help me find the truth."

She stood a moment, arms crossed, staring at her father, wanting to turn and walk away, to say go to hell to him and to her mother. "Fine," she said, knowing she'd caved but not ready to explore why she'd given in so easily.

She followed her father back to the benches and sat next to Jackie, who reached over and patted her knee approvingly.

"Your daughter and I just had a little talk about who you are and who she hoped you'd be. Do you want to tell us the truth now? Who are you protecting, Lisa?"

"I . . . oh . . . you're . . . damn you, Joe." Lisa put her hands to her face, a gesture Storm was beginning to recognize as a not too subtle attempt to keep from showing her emotions. After a moment she lowered them, looked from one to the other, then addressed Joe. "Fine. Yes, you're right. It's not about money."

Joe nodded encouragingly.

Lisa sighed, took a deep breath and said, "When I got sick, after Storm's . . . accident, I ended up in a homeless shelter. Several of them actually. The one I stayed at the longest was in a town called Walnut Grove. Yeah, I know, like that old TV show, Little House on the Prairie, only this town is near Sacramento.

"Anyway, there was a woman there named Alice. She was nice, showed me how to get along, helped me out. After I left, we kept in touch. She even came out and spent a week here last summer, after she got herself straightened out. She was addicted to painkillers, couldn't work, couldn't think straight. But once she could she went back to her old life, which was hanging out with a motorcycle club. She got a job working in a bar where she met those men." She lifted her chin to point toward the lodge.

"So, she told them about you, the handy location of your place, right off 101," suggested Joe.

"Yes, but not like that. See, we'd been texting, and I mentioned you were getting out of prison. She's always a bit paranoid so she immediately decided I should get a gun, so I could protect myself if you showed up. I told her it wasn't necessary, but I guess, in her drug-addled brain she was trying to save my life. She stole a gun from Bud, the older man. He caught her, and I guess there was hell to pay. Something about disloyalty and stealing from family.

"She called to tell me what had happened, but she was so upset I could barely understand her. I finally realized she was saying that they were going to kill her for stealing from them. That the only way she could redeem herself was to pay for her betrayal in some way that would benefit the club. The only thing she could come up with was to tell them the location of the lodge and that I'd be willing to act as a drop for their product."

"Oh Lisa," said Jackie, "I should have known it was something like that. Always taking in strays, no matter what the cost."

"Where's Alice now?" Storm asked.

"No idea. Somewhere in or near Sacramento I imagine. Someplace where other members of the club can keep an eye on her."

"We could try to find her, get her away?"

"This isn't some damned Jack Reacher novel, Joe," said Lisa. "We aren't young, and you weren't special forces or whatever. We're just going to have to—"

"What?" asked Joe. "Just go along to get along? That was me before Father Anthony, but I'm not that person anymore and neither is Storm."

"And speaking of Storm, maybe you should be thinking about her," snapped Lisa, "Why you dragged her into this in the first place is beyond me. What kind of parent are you?"

Storm and Jackie shared a look. They weren't part of this argument and were okay with that. Jackie smiled, and Storm smiled back, then said. "It feels just like old times." But it wasn't old times and Storm was astonished to feel a strange sort of buoyancy, a sort of happiness that she rarely felt except with Tom.

Was it the sudden realization that her parents were not monsters but were simply flawed and rather weak and damaged people? She was strangely comfortable with her parents nearby, a feeling she hadn't expected to experience. It felt good to sit here in the sun and laugh at her parents silly bickering.

But, Storm realized that despite her father's arguments, and her mother's admission of the truth, there was nothing she could do to help the situation. It was time to go home. Joe would have to decide whether he wanted to stay, head to Mexico, or catch a ride back with her.

"You two stay here and argue," she said, once again getting to her feet. "I'm going to take a walk and call Tom." She flashed a wide smile and headed back up the trail before they could respond. What she hadn't told them was that she needed time to develop a plan to rescue the dog. She wanted to approach them, see how they reacted, figure out if she could even get to the timid one without being mauled.

At least with that one there was a chance she could get him into her car. The other two might be an issue.

As Storm made her way back to the house her thoughts drifted to Howard, the first one who'd helped her with what he'd called justice killings. He'd been coldly calculating as he planned, decisive once he decided to act. He would have been helpful in this situation.

Her second partner, Lauren, let her passions control her. It made things more fun, but also much more dangerous.

She had considered telling her father about Lauren. How she was the byproduct of the drunken accident that had put him in prison. But Storm knew that though she could be hard, even brutal when she took vengeance for others, talking to her dad about Lauren would be too cruel even for her.

Lauren's passion or Howard's planning? That was the immediate question. For this, she'd have to adopt Howard's more cautious approach. No barging in to demand what she wanted, just calm, decisive action.

As she reached the edge of the garden and came in sight of the back deck she noticed that the men had company, a woman, who stood so close to Leon she was practically in his lap. He raised his beer bottle in Storm's direction. "Nice walk?"

"The lake is very pretty from up there," she replied.

"You haven't met our friend. This is Champagne," he said, but he didn't mention Storm's name. Storm didn't correct the breach of etiquette. Instead, she gave the woman a tight-lipped smile.

Champagne had teased golden blonde hair in a shade that matched her name, and the kind of pore-free skin one normally only sees in air-brushed faces on magazine covers. Her breasts had been so ludicrously augmented they looked like she'd blown up party balloons and stuffed them into the top of her tight black dress. They were even more noticeable in contrast to her tiny, Storm guessed, corset-trained waist. She was short and wore four-inch heels to compensate. They were cherry red, like her lipstick.

Both her name and appearance screamed porn star to Storm.

"You and your folks have a good visit?" Leon asked. Storm watched as he slid his fingertips provocatively along Champagne's side to the curve of her thigh and back again. She knew the mildly erotic show was for her benefit so she ignored it.

"We did," she said, an idea coming to her. "I've decided to invite my mom and Jackie to come stay with me and my family for a few days next week. She'll have to shut down the lodge. I hope that won't be a problem for you, or your friends," she said, gesturing to include the entire group."

For a moment the smile in Leon's eyes dropped and she could see the glimmer of something darkly malevolent, then the smile returned and in a carefree tone he said, "Well that works out just about right. Our associate will be here in a day or two and then we'll be heading out. I've sure enjoyed the time I've spent here. Your mother is a real nice woman. Gonna miss her, and this place. It's so far from town. You must worry about your momma, living way out here. It's so isolated and quiet" He took a sip of his beer, never taking his eyes off her.

Storm tilted her head to the side, gave him her sweetest smile. "I like it isolated and quiet," she said, then waited a beat before adding, "I wish it was even more so. People come by all the time. Probably more than you think. I hear there's a state park on the other side of the lake, and some farms just up the road. Cars drive by all the time. It can get downright crowded."

As if to prove her point at just that moment, Joe, Lisa and Jackie came into view and climbed the stairs to join them on the deck.

Leon introduced the trio to Champagne then said to Lisa, "We're heading out now, gonna grab some lunch but when I get back, you and I still need to have a talk about my friend."

Storm was happy to hear the men were leaving the lodge. It would give her the chance she needed to explore how she could rescue the dog. It would also give her another chance to talk to her mother about Alice. Maybe there was a way the four of them could come up with a way to protect Alice and free her mother from this situation. If not, well, she'd already decided it was time for her to go. She heard her mother say to Leon, "I'll be here. But right now, I'm heading to the kitchen to work on dinner."

"Well, if you're leaving I suppose I'll go find a garbage bag and start tidying up." Jackie pointedly looked at the collection of beer bottles scattered about, and the overflowing ashtray.

"Good idea," said Leon. "No one likes things messy." He looked at Storm when he said this. Then he and his crew got up and left.

Storm got the sense he had been trying to provoke her. It wasn't the first time either. There was something going on with him. Something subtle that she wasn't fully understanding.

"Need a hand in the kitchen," Joe asked. "If not, I noticed one of the rails on the front porch is loose. If you point me in the direction of your tools I could fix it for you."

Lisa said, "That's not necessary. I think you and Storm should head out yourselves. I can throw together something for the road."

Storm looked at Lisa but didn't know how to react. It was one thing to decide to leave, another to have her mother make the suggestion.

"I'm not going anywhere," said Joe to Lisa. "I've decided to stay right here."

"I already told you . . . "

Storm didn't wait around to hear the rest of the argument. She wasn't quite ready to leave either. Although she'd made up her mind to go home, she still wanted to see if she could rescue the dogs, especially the timid one. She went to the kitchen to sneak a peek in the fridge for food she could use to bribe the dogs. She doubted Perro fed them well. As she was stuffing some hotdogs into a zip lock bag she found in a cabinet she heard her parents and Jackie come into the dining room. She dashed to the french doors, down the entry hall and out the front door on tiptoe like a naughty child.

As she made her way across the lawn toward the dogs she thought about Leon and how he was using her mother. How he was forcing her to take part in his criminal activities. It was likely that he'd get caught and her mother would end up in jail. It was bad enough that one of her parents had done serious time in prison. What would Tom's family think if her mom were locked up too? What a silly thing to worry about. Tom's family already knew her family was messed up. Would they even be surprised?

Killing Leon sure would solve a lot of problems. Her mother's problems. Of course, she didn't really owe her mother anything, but Leon gave her the creeps, in a way only the worst criminals she'd dealt with had given her.

Besides, was it possible that she wanted to help her mother because she'd just realized she might not completely hate her? Maybe she didn't hate either of her parents anymore.

Lisa seemed nice. Look what she was willing to do to help a friend. Joe wasn't who she remembered. It was true he had been a terrible husband and father, and she wasn't ready to forgive and certainly she would never forget. However, as an adult she could also see that he'd been a man who got married too young, became a father too early and didn't handle it well.

As she drew near, the dogs caught her scent and came out of the shadows. They did not bark, and again Storm marveled at why they would train guard dogs to be silent. Because, she told herself, they aren't guard dogs. They don't keep people away, they punish people who get too close. They weren't trained to bark. They were trained to bite.

She slowed to a walk and a shiver slid down her spine. They reminded her of a child abuse case a few years ago. A man had tied his two young children to the back fence and set his dogs on them as a punishment for, God knew what. It had been that case that started everything. Punishing that man for what he did had been the first justice killing.

The abuser's name had been Jeffrey, Jeffrey Franklin Malino. She'd memorized it, as she'd memorized each of the people's names that she'd brought to justice.

There had been four rules: no blood, no bodies, no trophies and no connections.

She kept their names in lieu of trophies. Her only connection to what she'd done, and why. After Malino there had been Gavin Lester Everett, who burned his son with cigarettes. Then Helena Smith, a homeless woman living in an abandoned car, who kept her baby, not in her car, but beneath it so the crying didn't bother her boyfriend. There was Angela Ruiz, a mother who dated too many bad men, and Aislynn Clevidence, a nurse who tortured her patients by stealing their pain meds.

Others had died as well, innocents who got too close. She remembered their names as well, but for a completely different reason. She had always thought her father was a monster, but now that she'd spent time with him she wondered if she hadn't far surpassed him.

CHAPTER EIGHT

THE DOGS WERE chained up. The frightened one was still curled in a fetal position near the trunk of the tree it was tied to. The other two bared their teeth and growled low in their throats. She realized she had no chance with those two. They would tear her apart before she could unhook them. Even if she could, it would be a bad idea. Someone could get hurt. Possibly a child in the neighborhood. She'd be no better than Malino.

The dog on the far side was too far away to pose a threat. Luckily, the one on the near side had wound its chain around its tree and was only able to move a few feet toward her, which gave her some room to work.

Still, the way it strained against its collar with such fierce determination made Storm jittery. It's gold eyes practically glowed with hate and its lips were pulled back, showing sharp yellow teeth. Storm turned her back to it and felt the hairs rise on the back of her neck.

"Easy boy," she said softly to the timid dog. "It's okay." She mumbled a continuing stream of softly spoken words as she reached out and put her hand on the dog's haunch. Its skin twitched as if she'd hit it. "Poor baby, sweet baby,"

Behind her, the chain holding the vicious dog squealed softly as it moved back and forth restlessly. She tried to ignore the eerie sound and focus her attention on getting the fearful dog free. Hand by hand she worked her way up its chain to the tree trunk, where she found to her relief that it had been wound and tied there, not padlocked as she'd feared.

She worked at the knot until she got it undone then, taking up the chain so there was only about three feet between her and the dog's collar, she tugged gently.

"Come on, boy," she encouraged. The dog refused to move, curling even tighter into its defensive posture. She pulled harder and the poor animal slid across the fairly smooth surface of old leaves. Slowly she backed beyond the snarling dogs. The nearest one letting out a yelp of frustration as she moved from the leaf strewn ground at the base of the trees to the lawn.

"You shouldn't do that."

The voice startled her so badly she automatically reached under her shirt for the gun, a still unfamiliar weight between her breasts. Then, she saw that the man who'd spoken, Martin, was unarmed. She dropped her hand, nonchalantly wiping her palm on her jeans.

"What are you doing here? I thought you left."

"Obviously," he said, nodding toward the dog she was slowly dragging across the lawn. He smiled, a smile that lit up his dark eyes. "I changed my mind and decided to hang around."

"Well, I think you should have gone with them. I think you should mind your own business."

"And if I don't, what are you going to do little girl, shoot me? Or no, sic your dog on me."

They both looked at the dog, a hairy white c-shaped creature, trembling at Storm's feet.

"I'm stealing your dog," she admitted, and said nothing more, just tightened the chain and began pulling the compliant animal across the ground.

"Hang on," he said, and in a swift movement, scooped the animal into his arms. "Where do you want him?"

"My car," she said.

He followed her, and she unlocked and opened the back door. He settled the dog inside.

"I've got to roll down all the windows," she explained. She got in, turned the key to auxiliary and rolled the windows down several inches. She felt a breeze blow through and decided the dog would be comfortable.

"Won't your friends be angry that you helped me?" she asked Martin, who had walked around the car to stand next to her.

"Yeah, they'll be pissed. They'll be happy you're gone though, and if the price is one worthless dog, what the hell."

"Except I'm not leaving," said Storm defiantly. The curl of anger that had been simmering since her arrival had been ignited by his insulting use of the words "little girl". Suddenly the thing she most feared happened and she lost her temper.

"I'm going to call the police and have all of you assholes locked up," she snapped.

"On what basis?" he asked.

She wanted to slap the sneer off his face. "On the basis that you're blackmailing my mother into using her place for some sort of drug drop. On the basis that you're a bunch of worthless criminals who should be sitting in Pelican Bay. It's close you know, and the police would be happy to give you a ride there."

He smiled so calmly it was disconcerting. "At least we don't lurk in the woods and shoot people in the dark."

Storm's growing rage died as swiftly as a candle flame in a windstorm.

"Don't look so surprised. The minute Perro came running in with blood all over him my first thought was, well, the daughter's here."

"What? Why in the world would you think such a terrible thing?" Her protest of innocence sounded phony, even to herself.

"Why don't we go for a walk and clear our heads, maybe have a talk?"

Storm's uneasiness must have shown. He said, "Don't worry, you can always pull your gun and hold it on me while we talk." He looked pointedly at the spot where the gun rested.

A wave of apprehension swept over her. She felt vulnerable and exposed. For a moment she considered doing as he suggested, but she knew if she was able to get the gun free she was likely to shoot him on the spot. This was not the time. She had a lot of questions, so instead she just nodded and said, "Let's go."

Martin stepped back so she could get out of the car. She shut the door as softly as she could, so as not to scare the dog.

They crossed the road to a trail Lisa had pointed out when mentioning that people sometimes hiked or rode bikes around the lake. They turned left onto the path, the lake to their right, and almost immediately were plunged into the dark shadow cast by the moss draped trees. It was chilly and Storm found herself shivering.

"Here, take this," Martin said, taking off the jean jacket he wore and draping it around her shoulders. She almost shrugged it off, but the warmth was too welcome to turn down.

"We have a few things to talk about," he said.

Storm wanted to put off talking about shooting Perro to give herself time to gather her thoughts and sound slightly less panic stricken than she had. "Where did your friends go?" she asked.

"They went to the prison to arrange a visit with their boss this weekend. Pelican Bay only has visiting hours on the weekend."

"*Their* boss? Don't you mean *your* boss? Or are you trying to pretend you aren't one of them."

"Don't have to pretend," he said. "I'm a special agent with the Federal Bureau of Investigation and I've got my own boss to report to."

Storm shot a contemptuous look at the dark stranger walking beside her, caught him smiling at her in a way that was entirely too self-confident. "Sure," she said, her voice thick with sarcasm.

They walked a while longer in silence. Then Martin said, "Well, there's a complication I didn't foresee."

"What do you mean?"

"I thought we'd come out here, I'd bravely break my cover and you'd be dazzled and cooperative. It doesn't work if you don't believe me."

"Dazzled and cooperative?" Storm said, choking down a snort of laughter. "Why on earth would I believe you?"

"Good question," he said. "I suppose we could look up the number to the FBI offices then you could call and check with the aforementioned boss."

"What sort of cooperation were you hoping for?" Storm asked. She didn't think it would hurt to ask that question, whether he was an agent or not.

Martin pushed his hands into the back pockets of his jeans. Storm realized he was cold. She also noticed the gun tucked inside the waistband of his pants. "I want you to leave. Go back home to your husband and kids, and if possible, take your dad with you."

"And leave my mother here?" She didn't share with him that this was exactly what she'd decided to do just a short time earlier. Leave and then maybe come back after she'd formulated some sort of plan of attack.

"We'll protect her," he said. "We're not interested in her, if that's what you're worried about. I'll testify she was an innocent bystander, coerced into helping them. I won't reveal what that coercion consisted of and don't worry, I have no plans to reveal your activities. I'll make sure you're both safe. Of course, you may want to think about laying low, maybe even consider finding another hobby. This is going to result in some scrutiny of you and your family."

His words hammered into her consciousness and left her quaking inside like an aspen leaf. Was he saying he knew about the justice killings? But how could he and walk alongside her so calmly? Again the idea of going for her gun occurred to her. She could probably draw and shoot him before he got his hands out of his pockets. Then what? Roll his body into the lake?

"I have no idea what you're talking about," she said instead. "Do you think these bikers are using something they claim to know about me or Joe to keep my mom in line? That's ridiculous. My father's been in prison for years and I've had no contact with him. Same with my mom. Not prison, I mean," she said, flustered. "I mean I haven't seen her for years either. Had nothing to do with her. So how would she know about anything I have or haven't done?

"I'm starting to wonder about you. You say you work for the FBI and I'm just supposed to believe that? I'm pretty sure the FBI doesn't mess around with a few low-level bikers. I mean, you can arrest those three, but you know another set would show up to take their place."

"That's a very negative outlook you've got there, but you're right. There's always someone in the wings waiting for their chance. Still, it would be a lot of fun, arresting them I mean, especially if we can get the guy who's running them."

"Their boss, the one in Pelican Bay?" Storm conjectured.

"Yep, that one. He's the leader of the LOA, short for Leaders of Anarchy."

"Like that TV show?"

"Sort of. Sons of, Leaders of, it's all about the anarchy," he said with a crooked smile. "I think the TV show was based on the Hell's Angels. These guys are a spinoff of a different club that started in Nevada. They haven't been around long, but they've done well for themselves, the DOJ considers them a fledgling crime syndicate. They use I-5 and 101 along the coast running from Washington through Oregon and as far as Southern California. We thought once Blade was arrested they'd slow down, their network would collapse, but not so much."

"He's keeping things running, even from prison?" Storm asked.

"From a maximum-security prison," confirmed Martin. "He's got my boss pissed. See, we don't like locking people up and throwing away the key just to find they've kept doing exactly what we put them away for. It ticks us off."

"So you're using my mom--"

"No, we're using your mom's place. Leon right, it's a great location, isolated, run by two unthreatening women. It's perfect to breed a sense of safety, a place you might not only use for deliveries but for holding meetings."

"You're hoping someone important drops by."

"You got it," said Martin, and he stopped to break a small dead twig from an overhanging branch. He put it in his mouth, rolling it around like a toothpick. "Quit smoking two weeks ago," he explained. "Damn cravings."

"Who are you waiting for? How long is this going to take?" Storm demanded.

"Hey, I'm the one supposed to be asking the questions. But I guess I can tell you. We're hoping someone from the prison will show up. We need to figure out who's been getting messages out for Blade. We know Leon hasn't got the brains or the connections to run an organization this big, or this well-organized. You've met him, you think he's smart enough?"

"I don't think any of them are smart enough."

"Well yeah, there's that." Martin agreed. "Still, we figure Blade is either smart enough or crazy enough. He is definitely one seriously screwed up individual. In fact, he's so twisted they should have called him Corkscrew."

Storm saw that Martin was waiting for some sort of response from her, a laugh, a smile. She refused to give him the satisfaction. Instead, she gave him a deadpan stare.

Martin shrugged. "We don't name them, we just catch them."

Storm wanted to say, Well you haven't done a very good job as far as I can see. But she was too haunted by his earlier words. 'I don't plan to reveal your activities.' What did he know? How did he find out? Was he playing a game, hoping she had some sort of secret? Some FBI analyst mind fuck? Surely we all have something to hide. Until she knew exactly what he knew it would be better not to antagonize him. She gathered the edges of his jacket around her and said nothing.

"Hey look, a bench," said Martin, "and it's in the sun."

Storm saw that they'd come to a clearing that gently sloped toward a cliff, and a long almost straight drop to the lake, some thirty or forty feet below. A corrugated metal railing, meant to warn hikers of the abrupt drop, stretched for several yards along the edge. A bench had been placed facing the lake and a garbage can was chained to a nearby tree. This evidence of civilization and an attempt at order helped calm Storm's growing anxiety.

"Now, this is nice," said Martin. He sat down, his arms stretched along the back of the bench, his face turned up to welcome the warmth of the sun.

Storm sat stiffly, as far from him as she could, and watched a flock of small birds dip and soar, one moment against the washed out blue sky, another against the darker blue gray of the lake.

"You look worried," Martin said.

She turned to glare at him. "Wouldn't you be?"

"I suppose."

"Quit playing games and tell me what you think you know."

"Oh, are you going to keep it up with the heroic victim bit? Give me a break. Leon told us what you are, what you do. Your mother doesn't want the rest of the world, especially the law, to find out. Why else do you think a woman like her, with no criminal history, not so much as a parking ticket, would help him?"

"For Alice," Storm said, without much force.

"What?" He looked as confused as Storm felt.

"Alice, she's an old friend of hers. That's who she's trying to protect. But you know that. The LOA are holding her, using her to control my mother. It's all about Alice."

"Alice?" he said. Again looking so confused that Storm began to have her own doubts.

"She stole that gun," Storm explained, "from the old guy, from Bud. She got in trouble and offered up

Lisa's lodge like some sort of get-out-of-jail card. Leon told my mother if she didn't let him use her lodge he'd hurt Alice. Alice took the gun to give to my mother, to protect herself from my father, so you can see how she'd feel sort of responsible. She . . ." Storm's voice trailed off as she began to realize the truth. That the story her mother had told her about Alice was just that, a story.

Martin's perplexed look didn't fade, in fact, a furrow deepened between his eyes. "Well, you got part of it right, Alice does know Bud. She's his sometime girlfriend. But no one is holding her. In fact, she's in everyone's good graces. It was Alice that told Leon about you. You really think your mother would look the other way for the sake of a nasty little person she knew for a few weeks, years ago?"

Not ready to let Martin in on her suspicions, Storm said, "I think, if my mother's as good a person as you say, then yes, she would try to protect a friend, even a friend from her past."

"Maybe," he finally agreed. "But it's a lot more likely that—"

"So, they wanted to use the lodge because it's near 101," Storm said, interrupting whatever he was going to say, "which is what, something like a trade route?"

Martin nodded. "It's also near Pelican Bay so would provide a place to stay when they visited Blade."

"So, Leon and his LOA guys show up, tell my mother what Alice has done and threaten to hurt her if she doesn't cooperate."

"Which sounds good, except your mother was lying to you. None of that happened," said Martin. "There was no stolen gun."

Storm didn't know how to respond. She'd been surprised by what he'd said about her mother lying about Alice but she couldn't be sure. It still felt like he was playing a game with her, some sort of grand math puzzle. Every word she said gave him another piece of the puzzle. Once he had all the pieces the sum total of that knowledge could equal her going to prison. She had to be very careful.

Martin said, "Look, Alice wanted to belong to the club. She wanted a job bartending and they could make that happen for her. She told them about your mom's lodge and what she had on you. That's what gave them their leverage over her. You see, Alice was addicted to pain meds. When she finally got off them she went a little nuts and ended up in the Salem mental hospital. You know about that place, right?"

Storm realized then that the quaking sensation had returned.

"She met a woman," he continued to explain. "I'm sure you're familiar with her. She calls herself Lauren Barry. Claims she knows you very well. She told Alice that the two of you used to go out nights, bring justice to people who missed out on their fair share. She told her all about some couple, the Prentices, that you killed together. That's what she had on your mother. That her daughter, the probation officer, the wife, the mother of her grandkids, is a killer."

The silence in the meadow was broken only by the scampering of a squirrel as it entered the clearing, spotted them and ran for cover. Storm felt a kinship with it. She wanted to run, find a deep dark hole and crawl in. It was over. Everything she'd feared was happening. She'd be charged, convicted. Tom and the kids, they'd know who she was, what she'd done. She had believed that if she followed the rules . . . but she never had, had she, not really and her partners, Lauren, and Howard, they'd never even tried.

"Of course, no one believes her," said Martin.

"What?"

"No one believes Lauren. Everyone thinks she's crazy, because, well, she is, so they assume the story is just more of that crazy. They dismiss what she says about the basement, the Prentices, a woman named Celine."

The familiar names were a jolt. Storm covered by saying, "Yes, I remember, it was horrible, just horrible. She was truly insane and she fixated on me, dragged me into her world. I was lucky to survive her. I'll never forget the terrible things Lauren did." As she spoke, Storm unconsciously rubbed her hands together, feeling the tell-tale bump beside the nail of one finger. It was a small mark, like a brand, that Lauren had left behind.

"Yes, terrible things that a single woman, what was she, like five-four, a hundred and twenty pounds, could pull off. I mean, okay Celine, another small woman, maybe. But there were two of the Prentices, big, solid people in their own home. It doesn't play. I'm betting if we looked closer we'd find there had to be someone else, an accomplice. Leon sure thinks so. In fact, he's pretty sure Alice's friend Lauren is telling the truth.

"You see he noticed that the Prentices were on probation. It would be handy if the person who helped her had access to the client files of people on probation. Someone, willing to look up the addresses of abusers, share that information, maybe go along for the ride. I guess he convinced your mom you'd fit that role pretty well. I don't know why she believed so readily. That's between you and her.

"For myself, I don't know if he's right, but I do wonder, if we tested the trunk of your car, and everything in it, what do you think we'd find?"

Storm got up and walked to the rail at the edge of the cliff. She pressed her knees against it, felt the bite of cold metal. Blood, she thought. They'd find blood because as careful as she'd been she knew she hadn't been careful enough. Murder was messy, and she was no Dexter.

"They wouldn't find anything," she said, and turned to face him, letting some of the pent up anger and frustration of the past two days show. "Because there is nothing for them to find."

"It's okay, I'm not trying to trick you into a confession. I'm not looking into you or what you've done. Hell, I've read the Prentice's file. What they did to their girls. If I'd been there, who knows, I might have helped—"

"What do you want from me?" Storm asked, cutting him off.

"I want you to leave and take your father with you. I want to do my job."

"Leave my mother here alone to be used by Leon, by you?"

"I told you, we'll protect her."

"You won't. Your focus will be on Leon and his guys. I'll make a deal," She saw the tension in his face, and knew with a sudden flash of insight that he'd been expecting her to pull her gun. It startled her. Sure, she'd thought about it. But thought was not action. She'd never do that, never kill someone who didn't deserve to die.

As he slowly brought his hands out from behind his back she realized that he'd been ready to shoot her, kill her. She'd been cold, but now felt as if she'd bathed in snow melt.

"What kind of deal?" he asked, without missing a beat.

She took a deep breath and let some of the tension drain from her as she exhaled. "Let me and Joe stay," she answered. "We'll keep out of the way and if this company you're hoping for shows up and things get ugly we'll take Lisa, and Jackie if she wants, and go."

"How can I trust you won't just shoot me? I'm the one person here who can have you investigated."

Storm crossed her arms, staring at the ground as she considered how to answer his question. Finally, she looked up, locked her eyes on his and said, "I know you believe what they told you about me. I almost wish it was true. I think you'd respect that woman, but that's not me. Yes, I knew Lauren. Yes, for a time I did get pulled into her world, her delusions. It put my friends, my family and me in danger and I was glad when she was locked up. She's a big part of the reason I left my job. But the bad things that happened, that was her not me. I didn't shoot Perro. I've never shot anyone."

"Really? Then why did you take his dog? My theory is you were spying on the house that night, and you saw Perro do something. Maybe kick the dog?

Whatever he did it made you so mad you shot at him and as soon as you could, you took his dog."

"That's ridiculous," Storm said. "I took the dog because I went for a walk and noticed them tied to the trees. I thought it was weird that they didn't bark and I noticed one of them was curled up in a ball, shaking like a leaf. I knew all three must have been abused but he was the only one I could approach. He was scared to death of the other dogs, of me, probably of the wind. I decided to rescue him and I did. That's all there is to it.

"As far as what Leon said to my mother to convince her I'm some sort of psycho killer, well that's just nuts. I'm way too busy to go sneaking around killing people. I have a husband, kids, and until a couple weeks ago, a full time job. I can't control whatever crazy narrative is being spun but what I can do is stay here and do what I came here for, protect my mother."

"You honestly expect me to believe you're a poor, innocent—"

"I don't expect anything from you. You can believe that I'm innocent, or you can believe that I'm guilty. But you can't make me leave."

Storm thought how absurd it was that just half an hour ago she'd decided she was leaving. Now she was just as sure she would stay.

Martin gave her his twisted smile. She expected him to contradict her, to say that in fact, he could make her leave. She was surprised when instead he said, "You're not giving me a lot of choices here."

"No, I'm not."

"You sure you want your father in the middle of this?"

"He put himself in the middle of it."

"Interesting relationship you have with your folks."

"You don't know the half of it."

"We'd better get back before Leon does." Martin got to his feet and they walked side by side back up the trail.

"You'll have to leave the other dogs alone," Martin said, repeating what she already knew. Don't get into it with Perro. Don't push them into a confrontation. And whatever you do, don't reveal what I've told you about who I really am. If they suspect I'm with law enforcement and take me out, and I don't check in regularly all hell will rain down on you and your family."

"Now I believe you're a cop," Storm said. "I was waiting for the threat."

"No threat. I have a job to do and if you stay out of the way nothing bad will happen. I just need for you to behave."

Storm gave him her most disarming smile and almost believed it herself when she said, "I'll behave."

CHAPTER NINE

THE LODGE WAS QUIET when they got back. Storm took a quick peek in the car to check on the dog. He seemed fine, sleeping curled hard against the door.

She knew she should take the dog to a shelter but with all of Martin's revelations she felt now was not the time to leave. Remembering that she had a bag of hot dogs in her pocket, she fished them out, broke them into pieces, and dropped them into her car. The dog didn't move.

Maybe the men wouldn't even see the dog in her car. If they did she'd deal with it.

Once inside the lodge, she decided she needed to unwind, found a book and settled into the cozy chair beside the fireplace to read. She held the book open on her lap but after reading the same paragraph three times, realized it was impossible to relax when all she could think about was Martin's revelation that her mother thought she was protecting her. Their roles had once more reversed. It was a lot to think about.

At the same time, she was fighting an internal dialogue that urged her to leave everyone behind, get in her car, and run. There was no way Martin was going to let her go once this was done. He was charming, believable, probably very good at his job. And his job was being a cop. Arresting the LOA's boss was his mission but catching a vigilante would be the cherry on top.

Storm heard the rumble of the bikes, tires rolling up the gravel driveway and a few minutes later the front door opened with a bang. The LOA were back. They headed straight to the kitchen, through the dining area and out to the deck. Behind the bookcase wall Storm was happy to avoid their attention.

Soon she could hear them talking, their voices a low mumble, an occasional bark of laughter. She resented how they seemed completely at ease, not a care in the world. Lisa and Jackie were in the kitchen, Joe had gone for a walk, Martin had joined Bud, Leon and Perro on the deck. This constant inventory of everyone's location was becoming a new OCD habit. Though was it really obsessive compulsive or just good survival instincts?

She wondered where Joe's walk was taking him: to the high ground behind the house, to the trail around the lake, somewhere else? He said he'd been doing a lot of walking since getting out of prison. Some days he did nothing but walk, from morning until check in time at the halfway house.

Storm still had a lot of work to do to reconcile how she felt about him. She hadn't had the desire to think about it too much. To do so would mean tearing open old scars, looking straight into the pit where she kept her most violent emotions in check. Did she want to face those feelings or was it best to let the past be the past, refusing to allow it to control the now? The Willow that had been was gone. The parents she'd known then seemed almost fictional. Too bad her favorite therapist, Carol, had retired.

The woman, assigned to her when she left the hospital after the fire, never let her get away with easy answers. She'd always made Storm dig deep, even when it was painful. She'd told Storm that she was a late starter, that she'd earned her Masters at the age of sixty three. Storm figured she'd actually earned her skill as a therapist growing up black in a shitty little racist town in Maryland. She'd encouraged Storm to love her inner child, but to Storm her inner child was Willow, a pathetic coward who should have stood up to her father. Carol had certainly had her work cut out for her.

Suddenly there was a change. Storm didn't know what it was at first, then realized the tone of the biker's conversation had gone from light, pointless chatter, to loud, clipped and angry. At the sound of conflict her first thoughts were again, where was Lisa, Jackie, Joe?

Storm got up and went through the dining room to the kitchen, where she was relieved to see Jackie and Lisa sitting at the breakfast nook. They could all hear the raised voices of the men on the deck clearly.

"What do you mean you sold him? You can't do that?" Perro, was shouting.

"I guess I can do it, 'cause I did do it," Martin replied.

"Leon, you tell him. You tell him I want that dog back," Perro's voice took on a whining quality.

Storm moved into the kitchen entry and closer to the back door. Lisa and Jackie gave her curious looks. She shook her head and held her forefinger to her lips.

"You shut the fuck up, Perro. You don't order me around." Then: "What did you sell Perro's dog for?" Leon asked.

"What do you think?" was Martin's reply. Even though she knew his next words were for affect, they made her angry.

"You see her? How you think I'm gonna get in her pants? She wants a dog, she gets a stupid dog. Dog's no good anyway. Big chicken. What you do to it, Perro? Make it your girlfriend?"

Storm heard Leon laugh at the vulgar accusation.

"Come on. That's not cool," said Perro. "That wasn't your dog to sell."

"It was good money. You can buy another dog. Hell, you can buy five."

"Yeah? How much you get?" he asked, the tone of his voice dropping so Storm had to strain to make it out. "That's my money."

"I know. I was gonna give it to you. Hold on."

Storm realized Martin was probably reaching for his wallet. His lack of remorse combined with the offer of a payoff seemed to be working. It reminded her yet again that Martin the FBI agent was probably good at what he did. Given the situation, that was not exactly a comforting thought.

Lisa and Jackie, sensing that whatever had been going on was over, got up to check dinner. Storm left her post at the door to lean against the center island and watch.

"Maybe we should all eat on the deck," Jackie said, chewing on her lower lip thoughtfully. "It's been such a nice day and if it gets a little chilly we can turn on the space heaters." She'd looked at Storm while she said this so Storm replied.

"Sounds good to me. It's beautiful out there." Plus, she'd be better able to eavesdrop, though she didn't share that thought.

"It is, and pretty soon the deer will come through, heading for bed. We've got a couple little ones this year. They're so cute." Jackie turned back to chopping lettuce for a giant salad she was preparing.

"Clouds are getting pretty dark. Not so sure about eating on the deck," said Lisa. She stood looking out the kitchen window at the sky, unconsciously winding a loose strand of hair around her forefinger. It was one of her own nervous habits and Storm suddenly realized how much strain Lisa must be under and how good she was at hiding it.

Only moments after Lisa spoke they heard a long, rolling rumble and the men rushed inside. Beyond them Storm could see rain start to pour down, drops hitting the deck so hard they bounced back up. The smell of wet dust filled the kitchen. A dark cloud crossed over the sun, making the light and warmth of the lodge more significant. Martin closed the back door, and they all peered through the row of picture windows at the magnificent storm. A flash of light lit up the entire hillside followed by another boom of thunder.

"Joe's out in this," said Lisa. "I hope he has the sense to find shelter."

Storm's phone, in her back pocket, began to vibrate. She pulled it out and looked at the screen. It's Tom. "I have to get this," she said, raising her voice to be heard above the deluge.

As she moved past the dining area, back toward the fireplace and the chair she'd recently vacated, the sound of the rain diminished. She answered her phone.

"Hello."

"Stormy?"

The sound of Tom's voice was like a warm caress. Her heart slowed, and she closed her eyes.

"It's me," she said softly.

"How are you? You made it okay, I see. What have you found out?"

"I can't talk right now, but everything's fine."

"What's that noise?"

Someone had opened a door and the sound of the storm filled the house once again.

"Rain storm. It's pretty incredible. Wish you were here to see it. You know how they say raining buckets, this is more like barrels."

"But you're safe?"

"Yes, safe and dry. Sitting next to a fireplace actually. Very warm. Lots of atmosphere. It kind of reminds me of that place we went skiing last year, that place on Mount Bachelor, remember?"

"How could I forget."

"How are the kids?"

"They're fine. Miss their mother, of course."

The implied criticism wasn't wasted on Storm, but it didn't help his cause, if his cause was trying to get her to come home. "Why did you call?"

"To see when you were going to wrap up this mission and head home. We've got a ton of things to deal with and we need you here."

"I know, and it won't be long, just a few days, probably."

"A few days!"

Storm had been walking toward the front of the house, curious about that opened door. Now she saw her father standing in the entry, taking off the light jacket the rain had plastered against his shirt, and hanging it on a hook in the wall near the door to drip dry. As he moved toward the stairs Storm saw he was limping.

"What happened, Dad?" she asked. "You're hurt."

"Dad?" Tom's voice, was tinny, slightly garbled and filled with surprise.

"Hold on a minute," she said into the phone.

"I'm good, just twisted my ankle. Gonna get a hot shower, take some Advil, I saw some in the bathroom, and change clothes. Tell your mom I'll be back down in a bit, would you?"

"Sure."

She put the phone back up to her ear. "Hello. I'm back."

"What the hell is going on? Why is your father there? I thought you were going by yourself. What did you do, sneak out and make some arrangement with him after I sent him packing?"

"What?" Storm's immediate impulse was to throw the phone across the room, but she fought it and took a deep breath instead. After all, Tom had no idea what had happened, and she couldn't afford a new phone.

"No, no sneak arrangement," she said, as calmly as she could. "I saw him on the side of the road, trying to walk to California. I'm not so mean I could just keep going. I ended up picking him up and we drove here together."

"Well that's just perfect. A real family reunion, while the family who actually gives a damn about—"

Storm hung up on him. Then she turned the power off and slipped the phone into her pocket.

Upset, Storm wandered aimlessly throughout the house. The growing storm was a match for her restless energy. She was relieved when dinner was served. They ate in the dining room at two of the mismatched tables. The four bikers sat at one, Storm, her mother, her father and Jackie at another. Talk was subdued. It was hard to hear over the onslaught of rain and the rumble of thunder. Lightning lit up the windows randomly, like flashbulbs going off.

They all finished the meal quickly and after they were done Lisa said, "Jackie would you mind putting things away. I'll be back to help with the dishes in a minute. I want to have a talk with my daughter."

"No problem," said Jackie.

"Would you come with me," Lisa asked Storm.

Storm noticed that both Leon and Martin had looked up and were watching them. She pretended not to notice and followed her mother into the living room. Lisa stopped to take two throws folded across the back of one of the leather couches. "Take this, you'll need it," she said.

She led Storm to the front porch. The narrow roof gave only meager shelter from the rain. Lisa closed the door behind them. They each wrapped a blanket around their shoulders. The initial deluge was slowing but rain continued to fall and the wind gusted, blowing it sideways and sprinkling them with its icy touch from time to time. "Watch," Lisa said, and pointed across the road to the lake.

A sudden crackle of lightning sizzled across the distant sky and the lake mirrored the jagged white explosion of light. "Wow," said Storm. Her breath taken away by the beauty of the sight. Thunder boomed and a moment later another bolt of lightning lit up the clouds and the lake. They stood, side by side and watched in awe until the storm slowly moved away.

"I'm very glad you came," said Lisa. "But I think you should go. I'll let them use the lodge only until I'm sure Alice is safe. She's not very bright but her street smarts have got her this far. I'm sure she'll be able to get away eventually. When she does, she's promised to contact me and then I'll call the police. You don't have to worry, I can handle these men and once I don't have to protect Alice, believe me, I will."

Storm held back all the things she wanted to say. How she knew Alice wasn't in danger. How she knew it had been a lie. But, she figuratively bit her tongue and said nothing. It wasn't the right time. Instead she simply replied with, "I'm sure you'll do the right thing when it's safe. You're right, I should start thinking about going home. Tom called a little while ago and he needs help with the kids, with the move. There's a lot going on right now."

"The move?" said Lisa.

"Of course, how would you know? Tom's got work in New Mexico, a big contract, so we're moving there. I'll probably miss the rain, but a change of scenery sounds good.

"Well then, there's another reason for you to go home. But once this is all behind us, and once you're settled in your new home I hope you'll consider coming back, maybe bringing the kids with you. We have kayaks stored in the garage. Families love to take them out, paddle on the lake. I bet Lindsey and Joel would like it."

Storm heard the plaintive tone beneath the words and realized her mother was waiting, hoping for a positive response. This would be the perfect time to tell her what a horrible mother she'd been. To share with her how it had felt to lie in the hospital in pain, alone and afraid, abandoned by the people she should have been able to trust. This was the time to tell her mother how it had twisted her somehow and made it possible for her to become what she was, a vigilante, a killer. That if, someday she was caught and forced to abandon her own children, it would be her fault. In fact, maybe she was already caught in a trap of her mother's making.

The impulse to share these angry accusations churned within her with the intensity of the passing storm, but all she finally said, in a voice filled with civility and even kindness, was, "Like it. I think they'd love it. Maybe later this summer."

Lisa put her hand on Storm's where it rested on the porch rail. The contact was warm, intimate, alien.

"My gosh, your hands are like ice." Lisa rubbed her palm back and forth across the back of Storm's hand. "We'd better get inside and get something warm to drink. Hot cocoa?"

"Oh yeah. Hey, I'm gonna run out and check on that dog. I'm thinking the rain might be freaking him out, but I'll be back in a minute."

"Okay, I'll make some for both of us. Maybe Joe and Jackie want some too." Seeming grateful for something mundane and simple to focus on, she slipped inside. Storm pulled the throw more closely around her shoulders, and made her way down the sodden and somewhat slippery steps. With the windows partly down she hadn't bothered to lock the car's doors. The dog was lying on the back seat on the opposite side of where she'd last seen him. At least he'd moved at some point, and the hot dog bits were gone. She got inside and shut the door. The rain had slowed to a drizzle, but she didn't want to stand in it for long. She saw that rain had come through the windows, trickled down the inside of the doors and created damp spots on the carpet.

"Tom's going to love dealing with that," she said. "Also, this car smells like wet dog. You need a bath," she informed him. "Probably need to go to the bathroom too." She took up the heavy chain she'd left on the floor, the blanket slipping from her shoulders. Shivering, she pulled it back up. "You want to go out, fella?" She put one hand on the dog's back. The other she used to keep the ends of the blanket together.

She could feel tremors rippling under her hand and kept talking. "You're a good dog, aren't you, a wonderful dog. I'm going to tell Perro to go feed your brothers and maybe when he's busy doing that I'll shoot him and put him out of your misery. Would you like that?" she asked with rising enthusiasm and was rewarded by one wag of the long white tail.

She stroked the dog's fur, running her hand from shoulder to haunch. He lifted his head and licked her wrist. "Well, you really are a good dog, aren't you?" She slid her fingers across the wide head, stroking between the scarred ears. The dog shifted, a small movement but Storm took it as a good sign. "I think I'm going to call you Marty, after that Fed. He thinks he's got me all figured out. Do we think he does? No, we don't," she said, using the baby talk she never used around her kids.

"Wish I could keep you, Marty. Wish I could take you home with me, but you're not to be trusted are you. Your people messed you up, made you unpredictable. Can't have you around my kids, can I?"

The disturbing idea, that maybe *she* shouldn't be around her kids, wormed its way into Storm's thoughts. Tom would probably agree at this point. He'd put up with so much the past two years. Her late nights, the drama that had invaded their lives. She had let Howard, and then Lauren become part of their world, and now this.

"I'll find you a good home, Marty." The dog's ears rose, and she stroked his leg. "You like that name, huh. Good Marty. Good boy. Come on, we have to go for a little walk. She clipped the chain to Marty's collar. It took a little coaxing and a bit of dragging but eventually Marty climbed out of the car. She walked him away from the house, in the opposite direction of the trees where he'd been tied, waited for him to go to the bathroom, then took him back to the car. He lapped some water from a puddle then jumped back into the car as soon as she unclipped the chain, where he curled up against the opposite door. It was as if he were saying he appreciated the reprieve but didn't expect it to last.

"I'll be back with some dinner," she told him. "I promised to find you a good home. Now, I better go see if I can save mine." Pushing the blanket higher on her shoulders, she reached into her back pocket and pulled out her phone.

CHAPTER
TEN

ON THURSDAY MORNING Storm woke to the sound of her father's rhythmic snoring and the not unpleasant patter of rain. But it wasn't these sounds that woke her, it was bacon. Her stomach rumbled as the scents of breakfast cooking coaxed her from bed.

Sun was streaming through the single window, a warm bar of it across her thighs. She hoped it would be a nice day. That way the bikers would probably stay outside, coming in only for meals or to replenish their beer supply. Last night the weather had driven them inside, forcing more interaction than she wanted. They'd had the audacity to invite everyone to play cards. Only Joe had taken them up on it. Bud had even offered a pinch of Copenhagen, which her father, to her dismay, had accepted. The disgusting habit turned her stomach.

She'd slept in stretchy black capris and a long-sleeved jersey. Now, as quietly as she could, she gathered her clothes, took her gun and holster from the nightstand and slipped into the hallway.

After a quick shower she dressed in dark jeans, her hiking boots, a black t-shirt, and a blue and black flannel shirt. Layers, exactly what the capricious weather called for. She checked to make sure the flannel shirt concealed the holster once again tucked in her bra. It did.

She brushed her dark chestnut hair smooth then bent over and gathered it into an untidy bun held in place with a scrunchy. She reached into her travel kit and extracted a tube of dark brown eye liner which she drew across her upper and lower lids then smudged. Finally, she applied a coat of gloss to her lips.

She looked in the mirror then quickly drew the back of her hand over her lips, removing most of the gloss. What was she thinking? Who was she prettying herself up for? No one, she told herself. Putting on makeup was just a force of habit. She wanted to look good for Tom, but certainly not for anyone else.

Heading back, she met Joe coming out of their room. He nodded a greeting, scrubbed his hands across his face and mumbled, "Please, tell your mother to save me some breakfast. My God, I can smell the bacon from here."

"Me too."

Storm found her mother and Jackie in the kitchen, setting out covered bowls of scrambled eggs, bacon, and sausage links. A tray held toast and muffins.

"You really know how to do breakfast," Storm said with sincere appreciation, as she reached for a mug.

"Well, this is a special occasion. It's not often I get to make breakfast for my daughter." said Lisa with a warm smile.

Storm noted that her mother wore her hair down today, the light and dark gray strands falling below her shoulders, and couldn't help but stare. She wondered if her hair would turn that color, or would it be the more silver color of her father's.

Strange that she'd never pondered these simple things before. Not having her parents in her life for so many years, she'd forgotten about her biological legacy. At some point she should talk to both of them about potential illnesses. Was anyone in the family prone to cancer, diabetes? These were important things that she would want to know for the sake of herself and her kids.

There were heavy footsteps on the stairs and soon the rest of the guests filled the kitchen with their unwelcome presence.

"Looks good," said Martin, grabbing a plate. "Fancy spread. Guess having your family around is a plus for all of us."

Jackie pulled the tops from the bowls, giving everyone easier access to the food. As soon as the guests filled their plates they moved into the dining room. Storm turned to her mother. "How can I help?"

"Eat first, work later." her mother said, handing her a plate.

Joe showed up a few minutes later, wet hair combed back, morning scruff of beard now cleanly shaved. He filled a plate and joined them at the breakfast nook. . "You run a nice place," he told Lisa.

"Thanks, we try," she replied.

They chatted for a while. She and Jackie, her mother and father. They spoke about the weather, the best way to cook bacon. Storm was still surprised at the ease of their exchanges. Maybe it was the fact that the men in the other room gave them an enemy to rally against. Whatever the cause, there was a real sense that the four of them were aligned, allies if not family.

Storm was annoyed when the men returned to the kitchen interrupting their conversation.

"We've got somewhere to be," Leon said, as he and the men noisily piled their dishes in the sink.

"Maybe later we can fit in a little time for a bike ride." What do you think?" Bud asked Jackie, stroking his long white beard and giving her a lascivious wink.

"That's never going to happen," she said to the old biker, her blue eyes snapping, her lips drawn into thin hard lines.

"Oh, come on now, honey. You gotta learn to live a little."

She put her hand on her hip and was about to say something when Leon cut her off.

"Come on Romeo, the lady's not interested. We got things to do and places to be. Perro, you take care of them dogs this morning?"

"I'm going out right now, make sure they got plenty of food and water. Can't take care of Enzo. Don't know what she's doing with him." Perro shot Storm a look of unadulterated disgust, as if he were accusing her of starving his beloved pet.

She wasn't surprised. The worst of her offenders had always been able to rationalize their own actions, believing what they were doing was right, or at least done for a good reason. They never believed they were the bad guy. Yet, if someone else performed the same action they easily saw it as a wrong. She pointedly ignored the comment.

"Fine, but hurry it up, Leon said to Perro. Looking at Martin he said, "We'll be back in a bit. If Scott shows up give him the package and tell him what I told you." Then, turning to Lisa he said politely, "Thanks for breakfast."

Storm realized that once again, Martin would be staying behind. As the rest of the men left, the atmosphere became palpably lighter, at least to Storm, but then again she knew that Martin wasn't one of them.

Not for the first time, she wondered if it would be a good idea to tell her parents and Jackie that he was with law enforcement. It would certainly make them less stressed. But she'd promised Martin she wouldn't. He wanted everyone to act natural and she didn't know her parents or Jackie well enough to know how good their acting was. For now, at least, she'd keep it to herself.

Storm looked around the untidy kitchen then said to her mother, "Is there anything I can help you with?"

Lisa thought about it, then said, "Load the dishwasher?"

Grateful for something to do, Storm got busy, rinsing dishes and loading the dishwasher. Lisa and Jackie moved around the kitchen with practiced ease, prepping items for the next meal, tidying the counters. Joe grabbed a broom and swept.

When they were done Storm asked her mother, "Do you mind if I take some food to feed the dog?" I'm not about to dig around in their truck for their dog food."

"I should hope not," said Lisa, slightly aghast. "Besides, we've got tons of leftovers."

"Thanks, I'll go to town later and get some real dog food."

"Well, here, give me a minute to clean out the fridge." Lisa took a plastic bowl from one of the cupboards and filled it with a couple slices of left over roast beef, some sausage links and a strip of bacon. "Will this do?" she asked.

"Oh yes, that's plenty. Do you have a bowl I can use for water?"

"Sure do. We've always been pet friendly and it amazes me how many folks have left things behind. She opened a set of folding wooden doors to reveal a laundry nook. It held a side-by-side washer and dryer. Above them shelves were filled with cleaning supplies.

"This area is the pet zone," Lisa explained, gesturing to a pile of folded towels and a stack of bowls of various sizes. She took the top one, a ceramic bowl with a row of paw prints painted on the rim. Then she grabbed a rubber bone from a plastic basin beside it. "There's a few toys up here. He might like this one, but there's some tennis balls up here too. Maybe he likes to fetch? Anyway, help yourself to any of this stuff."

"Thanks." Storm piled the toys on top of the washing machine, then went to the sink to fill the bowl half full of water. She carried it back to the washing machine and tried to gather the rest.

"Here, let me help you," said Martin, appearing from the dining room. He grabbed the towel and rubber toys.

She hesitated a moment, then nodded. As they left the kitchen together, she felt everyone's eyes on them.

Outside, the day was bright with promise. Sun sparkled across the lake, creating an illusory path of glinting light. The air smelled fresh and puddles here and there reflected the trees and the bright blue, nearly cloudless sky.

Martin beat her to the car and held the back door for her while she slid inside. He climbed into the front passenger seat, turning sideways so he could see her while they spoke.

She ignored him, talking to the dog instead.

"Hey there, you want some water? She put the bowl on the seat. The dog had noticed Martin and was once again curled against the door as far away as possible. Storm managed to slowly coax Marty into giving his attention to the bowl. He sniffed at it and then ignored it.

"Here, try this," said Martin, handing the bowl of food to her.

This time when she offered the bowl Marty dove in, nearly knocking the bowl from her hands in his eagerness to eat everything in sight. It took only seconds before he was finished. "He needs a walk," she said, putting the bowl of water on the floor and taking up the chain.

"I'll go with you. Around the lake?" he suggested.

"Sure," Storm said. It wasn't as if she was about to argue with him. Besides she was curious. Were he and the LOA members the only ones who knew about Lauren Barry, or had he told his colleagues? Had his promise to keep her secret been real, or just a way to keep her in line?

The dog was reluctant to leave its safe retreat, especially with Martin nearby. Storm climbed from the car and gently pulled on the chain. "Come on, Marty," she said encouraging him.

"Marty?" asked Martin with a wide smile.

"I. It . . ." Words failed her, and Storm was surprised to feel a flush of heat across her cheeks. She hadn't blushed in forever. She turned her attention to the dog, ignoring Martin and regaining her equilibrium.

They crossed the road to the trail as they had before. The smell of pine and damp earth was pleasant. A light fog rose around their ankles as they walked, Marty, badly trained but growing in enthusiasm, ran back and forth from Storm to the end of his leash, tail wagging.

"He can't figure out what to sniff first," said Martin.

"Hard to believe it's the same dog."

"Guess anything responds to kindness."

"I guess," said Storm. So, what's up next for the LOA?" asked Storm.

"I told you. We wait."

"I'm not good at waiting."

"I gather your husband isn't either."

"What's that supposed to mean."

"Whoa there, don't get your hackles up. I overheard your phone call yesterday. Just seemed like you were getting annoyed and I figured it was your husband because you know, you said Tom at least twice. Do you know when you're pissed you turn Tom into a two-syllable word. T-om," he said, imitating her.

She couldn't help the laugh the spilled out. "Yes, so I've been told," she said, chuckling. "Well, I told T-om that I'd be home soon so I think we should do something to make that happen."

"Like what?"

"I've been thinking about that. I've been thinking this man they're waiting for would get here a lot faster if there was some urgent matter he had to deal with."

"Again. Like what?"

"Like, what if we take the package?"

"What package?"

"The package Leon referred to at breakfast. The one this Scott person is supposed to pick up?"

"Nice catch. But take the package? Are you nuts? I know Leon's been acting like a house guest, but trust me, he can switch that off in a heartbeat. Bud might be old but he's been involved in this game a long time and would kill you if Leon snapped his fingers. Perro's dumb, but he knows where his livelihood comes from. Plus, the LOA are up and down the coast, all it would take is a phone call and Leon would have a dozen bikers on your mom's front lawn."

"Sure, but wouldn't he go to his boss for instructions before he did that? Wouldn't his boss send those instructions by way of the man you're trying to find?"

"Not necessarily. Leon might feel he had to find the package and deal with who took it before going to his boss. He might not want to let Blade know that he'd lost the package. It would make him look incompetent, and believe me, he'd hate that. Think it through, Storm. It could go very badly, very quickly."

"I suppose you're right. Guess that's why they pay you the big bucks. Thinking things through and all."

This time it was Martin's turn to laugh.

CHAPTER ELEVEN

TAKING A SECOND cup of coffee into the dining room, Storm stared through the row of picture windows, just in time to see a row of deer leave the shadows of the trees and move down the slope alongside the house. Now she understood the tall fence along the back of the garden and deck. One of the does knelt and slid her muzzle under the fence, delicately nipping everything in sight. As she watched the rain that had begun as she and Martin returned to the house, slowed and finally stopped. A half rainbow shimmered in the sky for a moment and then was gone.

The LOA members came in late but were still served lunch. "Appreciate you feeding the crew," Leon told Lisa. She had started a fire in the fireplace and they seemed drawn to the crackling warmth. As soon as they finished eating they took over the table closest to the fireplace and started a game of poker.

Joe went for one of his now habitual walks. Lisa and Jackie went to work making bread and cinnamon rolls for the morning and Storm decided to drive to town for dog food.

She went outside. The clouds had returned and were moving across the sky like dirty gray sheep. A cool breeze and the damp made Storm glad she'd put on the flannel shirt. She took Marty for a short walk, then put him back in the back seat. She was pleased to see that he'd chewed one of the rubber toys. It lay on the seat in two pieces. She put on her belt, put the key in the ignition and turned it. Nothing. The car was dead. Battery maybe? She didn't know much about cars but she'd had dead batteries before. She'd have to call triple A. Or maybe her mother had jumper cables. Tom carried a set in his car and she'd always meant to get her own.

"Damn." Frustrated, she slapped her hands on the steering wheel, then realizing a show of temper was the last thing the traumatized dog needed, she stopped, told Marty he was a good dog and that everything was fine and got out of the car.

"My car's dead," Storm told Lisa. "Do you have any cables?"

"Yes, in the garage," she said. "Is it the battery?"

"No idea," said Storm.

"Where were you going?" asked Leon, standing in the doorway between the kitchen and great room.

"To town for dog food."

"Oh, Perro will get you some dog food," Leon told her. "No need to drive all the way to town. I have a mechanic friends who lives in town and will look at your car for free. I'll give him a call."

Perro had rushed out to get the dog food and returned with it in a plastic cup which he handed to Storm. He should have been annoyed, at least a little irritated. She had, more or less, stolen one of his dogs. Instead he wore a triumphant smile, and that smug look on his face told Storm volumes. She was going nowhere and her problem starting the car had nothing to do with anything as innocent as a dead battery. Leon had no doubt instructed Perro to disable her car, probably her mother's car as well. No doubt he'd enjoyed the task.

At first, Leon had tried to get her and her father to leave. Martin had made it very clear that they should, but they had not. Now it seemed leaving was no longer a choice. Storm wondered if it was because he had made the mistake of mentioning the package was here. He probably thought she wouldn't leave on foot, leaving her family behind. She wasn't sure if that was true.

That afternoon, Storm poured her third or fourth cup of coffee. She'd lost count. She was using the caffeine as a weapon against the drowsiness of the seemingly endless gray day. While everyone else had disappeared to their rooms upstairs, she stood at one of the dining room windows and watched as fresh sheets of rain washed the deck. Between the rails she noticed the colorful floats, bright spots against the gloom, and thought of Tom and the kids, bright spots in her life. She missed them beyond describing.

When she'd called Tom on Wednesday, his first words were, "Are you planning to hang up on me again?"

"No."

"That's good," he said, sounding as flustered and out of sorts as she did.

"You've got every reason to be mad," she said.

"Just don't hang up on me again. I don't like it when you shut me out. I hate it when you walk away, or drive away when we fight. There isn't anything we can't work out, if you stay and talk to me. "

"I'm sorry I made you feel shut out. I was just overwhelmed. Being here with my father and mother is a lot to deal with. I know you want to hate them, and you have every right to but I'm not sure that I do anymore."

"Well that'a huge change and you can't expect me to know what's going on when you're there and I'm here."

"I understand, but how many opportunities will I have to work out my past, maybe have a chance to forgive my parents and get to know them as people."

"I suppose that's true," Tom relented. "But could you maybe get to know them when we're not in the middle of moving?"

"But I timed this so perfectly, she said with her best evil chuckle. She could sense a lift in the tension between them and was grateful for it.

"What have you found out about your mother? Tom asked, shifting from anger to concern. "Is there really a problem?"

Storm had expected the question and prepared an answer for it.

"There is a problem, but it's being dealt with."

"By the police?"

"Yes," she was able to say in all honesty. "Yes, and it should all be over pretty soon."

"How soon?"

"I can't say exactly," Storm admitted. She could feel Tom's frustration in the stillness that came over the phone line.

"I see," he said, his voice so calm she imagined he was exerting tremendous control.

"Well, call me when you can." Then he hung up.

Storm had stood with the phone pressed against her ear, her mouth open to speak, but with no one to speak with. No wonder Tom had been angry about her hanging up on him. It was an awful feeling.

This had to end soon. She had to get home, smooth things over and start the new life she'd promised herself. She'd taken the first step and quit her job. No more client files filled with stories of cruelty and neglect prompting her to take action. From now on she'd just be Storm, wife and mother, gardener and maybe eventually, after a class or two, painter of landscapes. It would be an easy role to play, much easier than the role of vigilante.

She'd had enough of sleepless exhausting nights spent staking out an abuser's house, waiting to get inside, and bring justice for the greatest betrayal: that of a parent against their child. She had really believed she'd changed. Let the mission go.

Yet almost the very first thing she'd done was react without thought and shoot at Perro when she thought he was going to burn Marty with his cigarette. She didn't need files to know there was cruelty in the world. It was everywhere. But it was not her job to stop it and she knew if she continued she would eventually lose Tom and the kids. Her world would be empty of everything worth having. It was too high a price to pay, even for justice.

She jumped at the touch of a hand on her arm. "Oh."

"Didn't mean to startle you," her mother said.

"Good thing I just finished my coffee," Storm quipped, lifting the empty mug. "Or it would have been all over the floor.

"Wouldn't have been the end of the world," Lisa said. "Always something to clean in this place. Something to fix or paint or well, like I said, always something."

"You ever think of selling and doing something different."

"Never. I know I like to complain but I'd never give this place up. It honestly saved my life." She pursed her lips, looked uncomfortable, then said, "Anyway, not if I didn't have to. Oh, there's a few things I'd like to change. The back deck is nice but if I could afford it I'd put a big deck on the front too, where folks could sit and see the lake instead of a hillside.

"Joe offered to help you. I bet he could build a deck."

"Sure, he could build it, but where would the money for the wood come from? Besides, Joe's heading to Mexico."

"That's right." Storm hadn't given much thought to her father's plan to help Father Anthony and his kids. Funny how they might both end up doing something to help abused children, he with treatment, she with prevention. She smiled at the strange thought, but then became pensive. Where were these people when she was a kid? Were these the same people who had fought all the time and abandoned her? It was hard to reconcile.

"I hope he finds what he's looking for out there. Twenty years of his life gone," mused Lisa.

"Don't let yourself start feeling sorry for him," Storm cautioned. "He could have got out in ten, maybe even eight. There were no minimums for his crime back then," she explained, falling naturally into the role of probation officer. "It was his behavior while he was locked up that kept him there."

"I guess so, but still."

"No, you're right," Storm agreed. "It is a long time to be locked up."

"It's changed him. I can see that. He's quieter, more introverted, more thoughtful. Although I suppose that could just be age. We all change as we get older. I'm sure I'm not the mother you remember."

"No, you're not," said Storm, her mother's words eerily close to what she'd just been thinking. Physically though, Lisa *was* the mother she remembered. Maybe not the gray hair or the wrinkles, but the way she moved, the mannerisms and the words she used, they were all so achingly familiar.

Storm turned away, cleared her throat. "I think I'll go up to my room, gather some laundry. Can I use your washer and dryer?"

"Of course."

Escaping to her room, Storm sat on her bed. After a few moments she caught herself rocking. She hadn't done that in years. It was a self-soothing motion that one often saw in depressed of mentally ill people. Was she depressed? She didn't think so. Upset maybe. Worried certainly. The fight with Tom kept playing in some corner of her mind, a persistent buzz like bees in a summer garden. The apologies she'd made and the promises to be home within a few days had done nothing to sooth Tom's anger. An uneasy feeling that this argument might be harder to repair than previous ones was putting her on edge. She had to rectify it somehow, regain the comfortable, secure place that was her marriage.

When she arrived at the lodge she'd been sure she could handle anything. Now she felt distracted and, what was that old expression? Out of sorts. Yeah, that was it. She couldn't function at her best like this.

Forcing herself to move, she gathered the few items of clothing she wanted to wash then wondered if Joe had anything he'd like to have cleaned. She'd seen him stuff some clothes back in his bag that morning. She took the bag from the closet and put it on the bed, unzipped it and pulled out the bundle of clothes she found on top. They were heavier than she expected and there was something hard. She unrolled the clothes and was surprised to find a knife, and not just any knife. It was a serious weapon, a hunting knife designed to cut deep, and honed sharp enough to cut the fabric of the shirt it had been wrapped in.

She picked it up. It was heavy but nicely weighted. Her father hadn't walked into this completely unarmed. Storm was comforted by that. She took the soiled clothing except for the shirt, which she used to rewrap the knife, then returned the bag to the closet. As she gathered the pile of laundry she went back downstairs, unaware that she was humming softly beneath her breath.

CHAPTER TWELVE

AFTER STARTING THE WASH, Storm went back to her room and switched on the television. The local stations had nothing that kept her attention. She picked up the book she'd carried up last night and tried to read. It was useless.

Inaction was starting to get to her. She wondered if Leon and his men were as bored as she was. Surely sitting around waiting for someone to show up couldn't be very exciting for them. Or was this their job, riding their motorcycles from place to place, waiting to hand off and pick up mysterious packages, meeting with their boss? Where were their families, their wives and girlfriends, their children? The idea that they had children was profoundly disturbing.

She couldn't help wondering what the bikers were doing, where her mother and father and Jackie were. She knew she was being overly vigilant but she couldn't stop. Restless, she wandered downstairs.

Entering the dining area, Storm found the men were still playing poker. Leon held an unlit cigar between his teeth. Martin was laughing at something he'd said. Perro was building a tower with the poker chips Lisa had given them, which they weren't using. A pile of cash sat in the middle of the table. Bud had a beer in one hand and his arm around Jackie.

Storm did a double take. Yes, Jackie had pulled a chair up next to Bud and had her own beer. She wasn't actively flirting with Bud. She wasn't leaning against him or even looking at him, but she did nothing to remove the arm resting across her shoulders.

Oh hell.

Escaping the house, Storm found Lisa in the garden, perched on the edge of a raised bed, smoking a cigarette. Storm took an empty five gallon bucket, upended it and sat down facing her mother.

Lisa used her thumb to gesture toward a pack of cigarettes in the pocket of her shirt. Storm shook her head and said "What's the deal with Jackie? She's in there sitting next to Bud, drinking a beer. Did you see that?"

"Hard to miss. She's going on a bender, sure enough. I was kind of worried about that. A lot of beer around those guys. A lot of stress. Bad combination for her."

"We've got to get them out of here. You should ask them to leave and then call the cops."

"No cops. At least not yet."

"Whatever they told you, whatever is making you let them stay, you should know it's probably a lie."

"Can't take that chance." Lisa said. "Besides, they aren't doing anything wrong. They paid for their rooms and they aren't any wilder than other guest's we've had. In fact, rich folk's teenagers are usually much worse."

"How they're behaving isn't the issue. It's why they're here. Whatever they're transporting has to be illegal. You know that. It's likely something that will get you into a lot of trouble, and might even cost you this place." Storm looked pointedly around, at the lodge, the grounds. The beauty of the place was undeniable, the grass covered hillside stretching up to the timber covered hills all against the backdrop of a blue sky finally washed free of clouds.

Lisa nodded. "I know but we have to be patient. As soon as this person they're waiting for arrives they'll have their meeting then move on and things will get back to normal."

"Until the next time they show up."

Lisa shrugged, dropped her cigarette and ground it out with the toe of her shoe. "Until then I'll just take it day by day. That's what I've learned to do. You should go home. Your husband is mad and who can blame him. Go home and tell him you're sorry and make things right between you. You don't owe me anything."

Storm didn't know how to react to this comment. She also had a problem with her mother giving her marital advice, especially considering what a train wreck her own marriage had been.

For a moment she considered snapping some sort of sarcastic response, something about how her mother should fix her own life before giving advice, or that she had no right to give Storm advice after bailing so long ago, but she stopped herself. She wasn't all that sure of herself anymore. One thing she'd learned since Lindsey had been born was that being a mom wasn't what she'd thought it would be.

"I've noticed," her mom continued, "that you and Martin seem to be getting along. I've seen you out walking and talking, though I can't imagine what you'd have to talk to him about. I've seen him watching you too, when you weren't looking. You have to be careful. He's an attractive man, but he's also a dangerous, and as you said yourself, probably criminal, person."

Dumbfounded, Storm didn't immediately respond. What was her mother implying? Did she think that she was interested in some thug? That she would throw away her marriage for some guy she'd spent barely half an hour with? Storm was pissed but moderated her response.

She said, "You don't have to worry. The only thing we talked about was when I'm leaving, and will I be taking Joe with me. Seems like your friends aren't too happy about us being here."

"Friends? That's not a nice thing to say."

"I didn't mean it like that. Sorry, I'm in a bad mood today. I miss my kids. I want to go home."

"Then you should go. You don't need to be here. You've seen that these men are not causing any trouble. They'll wait for someone to pick up the package and then they'll go. Talk to Leon. Maybe he can get his mechanic here faster. He wants you to go, so I'm sure he'll do everything he can."

"Come on, Lisa, you can't be that dumb. Why do you think my car wouldn't start in the first place? Do you really think yours will? Our chance to leave is over. We know the package is here. They can't risk us telling anyone."

"Well, we'll promise you won't say anything. That they can hand over the package and —"

"Lisa, I don't honestly think this is only about the package. I'm starting to suspect that it's more about the meeting. They're using the package as cover. Why would they go to all this trouble to hand off a package. Why would they stay her for days? My guess is it has to be about this meeting.

"I bet they need a place where they can talk freely. What did Leon call it before? A quiet, isolated place. If you think about it, a place like that, also run by two women they believe are easily malleable, sounds like the perfect spot to me. They'll meet here. They'll use your place, and if it goes as smoothly as they hope, they won't stop. They'll take over. You know that, right?"

"No, I don't know that. The deal was they'd let Alice go if I let them use the house once. I'm sure they'll stand by our agreement. He gave me his word."

"I know you don't really believe that. You cannot be that naive."

"You're right, I'm not that naive, but how is you and Joe being here helping? You're just complicating things. There really isn't anything the two of you can do, is there? I want you to go home. I want to keep Alice safe. You and Joe want that too, don't you?"

"I do," Storm agreed. "But have you considered that maybe by being here we can make them reconsider their plan for using your lodge in the future? We're an annoyance, like sand in your underwear. We could turn up unexpectedly at any time. Maybe they thought you and Jackie were easy marks, vulnerable and alone. Now they see you have family, and we aren't going away."

"Sand in your underwear, huh?" Lisa said, with a chuckle. She rubbed at a spot between her eyebrows as if she were getting a headache. "I suppose you're right."

"You don't mind us being here, do you?" Storm asked, and the note of vulnerability she heard in her voice bothered her.

"Mind you . . . Oh no. Just the opposite. It's just, I don't want you, or your father, to make these men angry. They can be . . ."

"Not so nice," Storm finished for her.

From the house they could hear Jackie's laugh.

"Yes. Not so nice," her mother agreed dropping her voice, which had risen as they argued, to just above a whisper. "Anyway, it shouldn't be long. I heard Leon tell Bud he expected they would be on the road within the next two days.

"That's good news. Now all we have to do is pry Jackie away from them and we might get through this."

Dinner was pork chops, mashed potatoes and green beans. Everyone had drifted into the kitchen and now moved around the center island, filling their plates. No one spoke much. Jackie was trying to help, moving around the kitchen, every movement overly precise, obviously drunk but struggling for control. Storm was folding laundry, piling it on top of the dryer. Joe wrapped a pork chop in some tin foil and stuffed it, and a bottle of water in the pocket of his jacket.

"I'm going for a walk," he said.

"I'll go with you, if that's okay," said Storm.

"Of course."

"Just let me run this laundry up to the room and grab my jacket." Storm took up the pleasantly warm pile of folded clothing. She walked out of the kitchen, through the french doors and down the entry hall to the registration desk. Pulling open the top drawer she saw what she'd noticed before, a drawer divider, each section labeled with the name of a room and each holding at least one key.

She set the pile of laundry on top of the desk then took one of each of the room keys. She slid them into her pocket, closed the drawer, then grabbed the laundry and rushed up the stairs. She dropped the clothes on the foot of the bed in her room and then, without hesitation, tiptoed out and along the landing. She paused to look over the rail. The entry hall was empty. Digging the keys out of her pocket she moved to the first room, Leon's. The second key she tried let her in.

The room was similar to Joe and hers, a double bed, colorful quilt, antique dresser and wardrobe. Her reflection in the mirror above the dresser startled her for a moment, but she realized what it was and hurried on.

There was nothing on the bed, and only a watch on top of the dresser. Jeans and a shirt had been tossed over the room's only chair. She opened the door to the wardrobe. A box was sitting on a high shelf . Could it be the package Leon had talked about? If it was he certainly hadn't bothered to hide it. That carelessness spoke of their arrogance, their confidence that they had the upper hand. It made her angry.

She reached up and almost savagely pulled it down. It didn't weigh much and it was pretty small, about the thickness of two fat paperbacks. Tempted to open it she realized it would be dangerous to be caught here. Better to sneak it out and open it away from the house. Tucked under her shirt, the package, though small, would still be noticeable to anyone who saw her.

Carefully she shut the wardrobe, and then hurried out of the room, closing the door softly behind her and locking it. Gratefully she saw no one and ran on tiptoe back to Meadowlark. There she considered hiding the box but couldn't find a good place, so she put on her jacket and zipped it up. The extra bulk hid the box fairly well, and the drawstring hem kept it from falling.

When she reached the foot of the stairs, Storm shouted to her father, "You ready to go?" Her heart was pounding and she only hoped that her voice sounded normal.

"Yep," Joe said, and the french doors opened. Behind him, stood Martin, and he swept her face with such a questioning gaze that it felt as if he were trying to peel away the layers of her skin and reveal all of her secrets.

She managed a wan smile.

Lisa moved past Martin and stood beside Joe in the doorway.

"We're going for a walk," Storm told her, grateful she could address her and not Martin, who seemed able to peer too deeply into her intentions. "We'll be back soon," she said hoping to reassure her mother that she wasn't being abandoned.

Lisa looked worried, but she too hid behind a phony smile. "Good. It'll be dark soon. When you get back you can help me make dessert for the rest of the week. I'll get some canned apples and what not out of the pantry."

Outside they found the evening unusually warm. The sky was turning dark near the horizon as the planet slowly spun them away from the sun. As they walked through the old orchard the scents of rotting apples and the ocean made an oddly nice combination. As they approached the two benches Storm's father said, "Do you want to stop here, or keep going."

"Keep going," was her immediate reply. It felt good to be outside and moving. At home she ran every morning and most evenings, a habit that grounded her, gave her time to think. At home she had many routines but here everything was about waiting and anticipating. Storm hadn't realized how tense she was until she began to relax as they drew farther from the house.

If not for the hard corners of the package tucked in her jacket and poking her in the ribs she might have been able to enjoy herself more. But it was less the thing's physical presence than its contents that bothered her.

They walked to the edge of the road, checked for traffic, which was non-existent, and crossed. Under the redwoods it was cold and damp. They kept moving, until looking back they could barely see the roofline of the lodge. At the next clearing, Storm found a fallen log and they sat on it, though it was spongy and rather damp. Ignoring that, she unzipped her jacket, removed the box and held it out.

"Oh damn, Willow, is that what I think it is?" Joe asked.

Storm nodded, choosing to ignore the use of her old name, and looked more closely at the box. It was wrapped in brown paper, taped at two ends.

"I don't think I can open this without making it obvious," she said.

"Here, let me try," he said, fishing a small folding knife from the front pocket of his pants. He took the box, rested it on his thigh and carefully slid the blade under a loose edge of tape.

Storm watched the delicate procedure with growing frustration. She would have ripped the cover off, but knew if she wanted to return the box without them knowing she'd taken it, his way was better.

Finally, he was able to unfold one of the ends, reach in and carefully pry open the box. Storm bent close, expecting to see pills or powder. Instead she saw semi-transparent green plastic bodies and silver USB ports. The box was filled with flash drives. Dozens of them. She reached in and took one out. The small device was completely common and gave no clue as to what it contained. She turned it over looking for a label but there was none. She looked at her father and saw he wore the same puzzled expression she must be wearing.

"They aren't moving drugs," she finally said.

"More like information," her father agreed.

"What kind of information? It can't be good, whatever it is."

"I don't know. My first thought was corporate espionage, then I thought, maybe state secrets, or I don't know, plans for a nuclear warhead. But maybe I've watched too many movies."

"Me too."

They sat in silence for a moment, each staring at the bit of plastic and metal resting in the palm of Storm's hand.

Sighing, Storm slid the flash drive into her pocket, then took up the box and began rewrapping and taping it.

"What are you doing?" her father asked.

"We need to get this box back before they notice it's missing but we also have to see what's on these. I'm all fumble fingered. Can you put the cover back on better than this?"

"I think so." He bent to the task, studiously folding the paper and smoothing the tape down with his thumb. "Looks okay to me."

"Me too. Let's head back."

"Okay, but give me the box, tell me where you found it. I'll put it back."

"What? No, I'll do it. I can hide it under my jacket. You didn't even notice it was there."

"Doesn't matter. I can hide it too, plus I'm older. They won't wonder that I have to go to the bathroom the minute I get back after a short walk. It'll seem natural."

"That's ridiculous. They aren't going to analyze your bathroom habits."

"You don't know that." He tucked the box into his jacket.

She sighed. "Fine. You win." Taking out the key to Leon's room she handed it to him.

While they walked back to the lodge Storm explained exactly where Joe should return the box but her thoughts were on the small device in her pocket. A thing that weighed so little she couldn't even tell it was there, yet whose importance could be enormous.

CHAPTER
THIRTEEN

THEY CAME OUT OF the woods directly across from the lodge. Both thought the men would be back at their favorite place, the back deck, so they decided to enter at the front.

They climbed the front stairs and going inside found the lodge quiet, with only the hum of the dishwasher from the kitchen disturbing the silence.

Joe looked upstairs then back at Storm, who nodded. As Joe hurried up the stairs, Storm took off her jacket and hung it on one of the hooks by the front door, taking her time. She would be her father's lookout and wait until he came back down the stairs, then she'd find her mother and ask what kind of dessert they were making. It would be the kind of innocent question one would ask.

The sudden sound of raised voices from upstairs made her stomach clench She rushed up the stairs, using the handrail to propel herself faster.

She reached the landing just in time to see Joe thrown backward and slammed into the railing which shook at the impact. Leon erupted from his room, fists swinging. His right connected, and Joe went to his knees.

Storm charged. Her body slammed into Leon and he staggered sideways but didn't fall. Instead he twisted and threw a punch. She drew back just in time and his fist slid past her cheek. Someone grabbed her from behind. As she struggled against the restraining arms wrapped around her, Leon delivered a hard backhand that caught the right side of her face. The blow stung. Enraged, Storm kicked with both feet, letting the man holding her carry all of her weight. She caught Leon in the stomach and he staggered back into the railing. She tried to kick again but the man holding her wrapped one arm around her neck and drew her head back. Suddenly she was choking, fighting for air.

Leon came at her, aiming a punch at her midsection, but she managed to twist away just in time and the blow landed on her hip. Managing to kick out again, this time catching Leon's wrist with the tip of her boot. The look of pain on Leon's face was gratifying.

"Stop fighting," she heard Martin whisper harshly, and she realized it was he that held her, drawn hard against him, his forearm against her throat, still cutting off her breath.

From downstairs Lisa shouted, "What's going on up there?"

Leon ignored the question. His attention had turned to Joe, who was using the railing to leverage himself to his feet.

"You stay put, old man," Leon said, clasping his injured wrist with his other hand. Unfortunately, it wasn't too badly injured as less than a second later he was able to pull a handgun from a holster under his jacket.

He pointed it at Storm, matte black and lethal looking. As she stared into the dark muzzle time seemed to slow down. She felt a drop of sweat slide from her hairline to her temple and down past her ear. Joe knelt where he was, frozen on one knee, watching as Leon kept the gun pointed at Storm, the muzzle turning in small, irregular circles.

"Get her gun," he commanded.

Martin released his grip around Storm's arms, then slid his right hand under Storm's shirt to the holster between her breasts. As the tips of his fingers slid across her sweat slick skin Storm's mind raced. Was he still playing his role, or was he actually one of them? Should she push his hand away, try for her gun? Her body trembled. He loosened the grip on her throat, then tightened it again, then loosened it again. What was he trying to tell her? He tugged her gun free from its holster, and then held it out to show Leon. The familiar sight of her Glock 17 begged that she reach for it, but she fought the suicidal impulse.

"I've tried being a nice guy," said Leon. "A good guest. Lisa's been a good host and Jackie, well Jackie does as she's told. No one invited the two of you to the party."

Martin let the hand holding her gun drop, almost casually, against her right thigh. He loosened the grip around her neck but stayed close. Stay calm, he was trying to tell her she realized. Don't do anything stupid.

Storm heard footsteps on the stairs. "Stay the hell down there," Leon shouted.

The footsteps stopped.

"As I was saying, no one invited you. At first I even did my best to send you packing. I thought having Martin hit on you would be enough to convince you to leave, but I guess not, I guess maybe you liked it? You and that Jackie chick. Couple of sluts is what you are. Lonely sluts." Leon gave Storm a salacious wink.

"Then you got all nosy. Hung around listening, asking questions. I decided okay, make them hang around until my business is done and then we're out of here."

Storm thought about how what she'd told her mother was right. That Joe and her, by just being present, had made the lodge less comfortable to use and made it less likely they'd want to use it in the future. She didn't have time to feel pleased with herself however.

"But now," Leon was saying, his tone becoming more clipped, more angry. "But now you have crossed a line. You have gotten into my business and I won't stand for it."

"What are you talking about?" Storm asked, hoping to break the rising tension. "What business?"

"Playing stupid doesn't fit you, somehow," said Leon. I'm talking about the business of the box the old man took from my room before you two went on your little walk. The box he just returned after you two snooped through it. This is not good manners. I'm surprised your mother didn't teach you better."

Joe said, "She didn't know anything about—"

Leon's almost casual kick to Joe's side was brutal. Joe hunched over, grasping his stomach, his mouth opening and closing like the gills of a beached fish.

"Stop it, you son of a bitch," Storm spat as he drew back his booted foot to kick the older man again.

"You want me to stop, fine," said Leon and didn't follow through with the kick. "Then let's go downstairs and have a little chat. Martin, help your lady friend downstairs." He gestured with the gun but Storm stood her ground ignoring the increasing pressure as Martin pressed against her.

"What about my father?"

Leon smiled, "Such love, such sacrifice. Get up old man, your kid wants to protect you."

Joe got to his feet a bit unsteadily then limped heavily toward the stairs, one arm wrapped around his rib cage. Storm wondered if the kick had broken his ribs. If a shattered edge was cutting into a lung. Feeling defeated, she followed him down the stairs.

"Everyone into the dining room," Leon commanded.

Storm saw Lisa standing a third of the way up the stairs, eyes wide with anxiety. Behind her were Jackie and Bud.

"Ladies," said Bud, and gave a sort of curtsey, swinging his arm in what Storm supposed was his idea of a gallant gesture.

In the dining area, Leon gestured toward a table and while they took seats he stood, arms folded, the gun still in his hand, his finger resting alongside the trigger guard. Storm wondered if she could take it from him, shoot him, then Bud, maybe even Martin.

She tried to focus on something else before the thought became an impulse. Where was Perro, she wondered. Was he standing by somewhere, waiting to step in if one of them tried something?

Lisa had chosen a chair beside Storm and now took her daughter's hand, entwining her fingers through Storm's. Wanting to keep her hands free, Storm nearly pulled her hand away. Her father sat on her left. Across the table sat Bud, and to his right, Jackie, who appeared to be sleeping with the enemy, the traitor. She wore the glazed look and slightly vacant smile of someone who'd had way too much to drink. The chair to the left of Bud was empty as were the chairs at the head and foot of the table.

"Here's what we're going to do, people," Leon said slowly and calmly. "We're going to wait around for a friend of mine to visit. When he arrives we're going to have a pleasant evening. Lisa and Jackie are going to cook us a fancy meal. Joe is going to be our waiter. Storm is going to stay in the kitchen, do dishes, mop the floor and all that kitchen shit. But don't worry, you'll have Perro to supervise you. As a matter of fact, when he gets back from the grocery store I'm going to give him a gun. I think he's earned it. Perro as a supervisor. Yeah, he'll be tickled."

"And what if we say no?" asked Lisa, her fingers tightening around Storm's.

Leon's tone changed from phony friendly to honest hostility. "You won't. You have too much to lose. You see," he said, addressing Storm. "We know all about you. Tell her, Bud?"

Bud leaned back in his chair and stroked his beard like an old story teller preparing to launch into his favorite tale. "Well see, I've got a gal back in San Francisco, her name's Alice. Sorry, hon, he told Jackie, and patted the back of her hand. She likes drugs like you like booze. Once in a while she has to go get dried out. Last time she ended up checked into the state nut ward up in Salem. Had a roommate, called herself Lauren Barry."

Fear flowed through Storm like high mountain rain, cold as ice. She fought to keep her emotions hidden. Beside her Joe sat up straight. Groaned at the pain it caused.

Bud smiled at the expression on Joe's face at the mention of the name. "I see you've heard of her. She had an interesting story to tell Alice. A story about a woman named Storm. A woman who was a probation officer by day, and a stone-cold killer by night. This Storm was a card-carrying vigilante. A good one too. Never got caught. Never even got looked at hard. But you gotta wonder if the cops did look, how long would it take for them to figure it out?"

Bud looked directly at Storm. He made her think of an evil Santa Claus, with a mean twinkle in his hard gray eyes and the yellow snuff stains in his otherwise white beard. "I don't think it would take too long," he continued, "and they'd be carting her off to prison.

"Saddest thing is how she'd be leaving behind a husband, two sweet kiddies, not to mention her mom and pop. Didn't know about pop until he showed up but hell, can't be expected to know everything. We knew about mom because Alice told us all about her. Lady who had a big old lodge out in the middle of nowhere, but right where it would be handy. The boss," at this Bud gave a nod to Leon, "he didn't have to think too long. He'd call up, make a reservation. Once he got here he took Mom aside for a little business talk. Boss can be pretty convincing. Talked Mom into letting him hold a meeting here now and then, drop off a package. Not much to ask for keeping his tongue. Not much at all, is it Mom?"

"My name is Lisa," Storm's mother said softly but firmly. "And no, it's not too much to ask, given what you *think* you have on my daughter, but I never agreed to you hitting Joe or holding a gun on anyone. Is this the way you're going to honor our agreement?" she said, addressing Leon. "Maybe *your* boss won't be too happy about that."

"I'm pretty sure he'll be happy that's all we did," Leon told her, "given that your ex took it upon himself to search my room, probably all of our rooms, and took something that didn't belong to him."

"I put it back," Joe argued. "I wasn't going to keep it. Hell, I don't even know what those things are?"

"You don't know what they are?" Leon asked, his voice filled with doubt.

"Well, I mean, sure I know what they are, I just mean I don't know what's on them."

"You didn't put one in a computer and take a quick peek?

"No, I didn't. How could I? I took the box with me and went for a walk in the woods. There aren't any computers in the woods."

"Well, that's something. What the hell did you think you were gonna find in that little box?"

"Honestly? Drugs. Cocaine or pills or something. I wasn't going to take any, I just wanted to know."

"Just curious, huh?"

"You know, curiosity killed the cat," Bud said. "Ain't that right, babe?" he asked Jackie.

"Thas right," she told him with a wide smile, the bottle of beer in her hand swaying.

"So do you know anything now, anything more than you did before you took it?" Martin asked, ignoring Bud.

Joe shook his head, lowered his eyes to the table and took on that same beaten dog expression Storm had seen before. "No, I don't. I thought maybe some kind of designs, a patent or something. Hell, I don't know what's worth money nowadays. Besides, it's none of my business."

"You got that right," Leon said, and slid his gun into its holster. Storm imagined she felt a level of tension drop from him. "You think you can remember that?" he asked. "You think you can all remember this is none of your business?"

Everyone nodded or mumbled their agreement. Storm heard her father say, "Yes, sir." Leon heard it too.

"Sir. You hear that? Now that's the way to show respect. Lisa, you think you can keep your family in line for just a little longer? Company will be here on Saturday and after that we'll be cutting out. We'll keep shut up about your daughter and what we *think* we have on her, you'll keep your mouth shut about what you *think* you have on us. After a few weeks we might call and rent some, or maybe all your rooms for a few days. It'll go just like this, but without all the drama. You'll get paid. Any problems with that? Any of you?" he asked, looking pointedly at Storm and her father.

They both shook their heads.

"What did you say?" he asked, cocking one ear toward Storm.

"No, no problems," Storm said.

"No problems, Sir," Leon corrected her.

"No problems, Sir," she said through clenched teeth.

"No problems, Sir," agreed Joe.

"Good, now just to be sure we all remain good little boys and girls, how about we put our cell phones on the table. Don't worry, you'll get them back when we leave" he said unconvincingly.

Storm placed her phone on the table. No one else had one.

"You kidding me? None of you has a cell phone?"

"We use the landline," said Lisa. "We're too poor to buy fancy phones."

"Never liked them," said Joe.

"You are an odd bunch of people," Leon said, pocketing Storm's phone. "Now how about everybody going about their business. Martin, stay here, I want to talk to you a minute."

No one moved until Martin slammed his fist on the table and said, "Go."

Leon smiled his approval as Storm and her family hurried to comply.

While Martin and Leon huddled in the living room, Bud led Jackie upstairs. Storm watched the woman's blatant display of disloyalty with disgust. Storm and her parents stood woodenly in the kitchen.

No one spoke for a moment. Storm was processing what Bud had revealed and getting her head wrapped around it. It explained her mother's actions better than all the half-truths.

Storm wanted to say something, deny what Lauren told Alice, but she didn't say anything and in her silence felt she substantiated what Bud had told them.

Joe seemed the most shocked by Leon's revelation. Which made sense given he'd just learned about it while Lisa had known for some time. He was the one who finally broke the silence. Unexpectedly he turned to Lisa, "You're letting these men use your bed and breakfast based on some lies someone told them about our daughter. That girl, that Lauren Barry, she's the girl I hit with my car. I didn't know she ended up in a mental ward. But if she was there, it was for a reason, right? She must be unwell. She must hate me and Storm's my daughter so she must hate her too, right? To tell people that Storm's a killer, a vigilante?" He gestured toward Storm as if the very sight of her was proof that it couldn't be true.

"I'm a killer?" Storm asked, hoping she was doing a good job of looking stunned. "Why on earth would you ever think that?" She tried to turn it into a joke. "I mean seriously, I've got two kids, a husband and up until two weeks ago, a full-time job. Where would I find the time?"

"Of course you're right," Lisa said, directing her words to Joe. "I don't know what I was thinking. They just threw all these accusations about her at me, just knocked me off my feet. I guess I haven't had time to think about how insane the very idea is."

Storm turned away, looked through the kitchen window. Her mother was lying for her now. It should make her happy, having her mother in her corner, but the good feeling she got from the proof of her mother's caring was outweighed by her sense of dread.

It was all unraveling, the way she'd always suspected it would. She'd written four rules to keep her free from prison but she and the two people who'd helped her had broken those rules, they'd used weapons, left a trail of blood, connections and bodies. Sensing her father staring at her, searching for an answer, she could feel the walls going up around her emotions. The old protections falling into place.

"We should clean up that lip, and get you some ice. It's starting to puff up," Lisa said to Joe, "and there's a little blood on your chin. Storm, could you go into the downstairs bathroom? There's a medical kit under the sink. We need a bandage so we can wrap Joe's ribs. While you do that I'll clean him up."

Storm nodded and went to find the bandage, grateful that her mother was taking charge and thankful for a task to do.

CHAPTER FOURTEEN

FRIDAY WAS A DAY of waiting and thinking. The worst kind of day. Everyone was subdued but tense. It was obvious Leon had his men on a tight rein. For one thing, Storm noticed they weren't drinking, not even Bud followed his morning coffee with the usual beer chaser.

Jackie looked tired, her pixie hair spiked on one side as if she'd woken that way but hadn't bothered to do anything about it. Joe had a decided limp from his fall, his lower lip was puffy and there was a bruise on his chin. His ribs seemed better and his breathing was normal. Probably only bruised not broken they'd decided. Only Lisa seemed like herself, moving through her morning routine of making breakfast and prepping lunch.

After Joe was talked into eating a light breakfast, he got Lisa to help him put together an ice bag then headed upstairs to rest and ice his swollen knee. Storm envied his escape. She felt jumpy. For a moment she considered going for a run to burn off some of the stress but at this point would Leon actually let her leave? Besides, she didn't want to leave her parents alone with Leon and his thugs, the four bikers seemed especially on edge.

The weather wasn't helping, the coastal fog Storm was beginning to get used to was refusing to burn off and in the distance dark clouds promised another rain storm. Going outside meant standing in a steady mist that slowly gathered on your skin and clothes. Once they realized this, the bikers settled inside but instead of hanging out together they appeared to each want their own space.

After a while Perro went outside, headed toward his truck. Storm took the trash out to the garbage bin out front, as an excuse to see what he was up to and to make sure he didn't get near Marty. At first, she thought he was going to work on his truck, clean it maybe, but instead he sat in the cab, staring at something in his lap. Maybe he was reading she thought, though she hadn't pegged him as a reader.

Martin came up behind her on the landing, looked over her shoulder at Perro in his truck. "He does crossword puzzles," he told her. "He either thinks it makes him look smart or maybe that it will make him smart. Not sure which."

"You think we should go?" Storm asked. "Me and Joe, take off, maybe hide up in the hills. Good view of the lodge from up there."

"Too late," he told her. "It would just make Leon mad and he's already at the boiling point. Might not play out so well for the folks you leave behind. Besides, this will be over soon. Someone could even show today. He hasn't said it, but I think that's what he's expecting."

"But he said Saturday."

"Yeah, he does stuff like that. Likes to misinform and keep you off track. But I'm pretty sure the meet's going to happen soon, today or the next day is my best guess."

"This meet, who do you think it's with?"

"I'm guessing a corrections officer, someone who works at Pelican Bay and has been carrying messages, and orders, from Blade to his crew. We find out who he is, get him to confess and then we drop Blade down a hole so deep no one will ever hear from him again."

Storm rubbed her arms. The damp cold was creeping in. "Mom was right, she needs a bigger deck out here, with a roof."

"If I put my arms around you, don't freak out. Don't fight. If anyone sees us talking I want it to look like we're *real* friendly. Leon asked me to try to, well, seduce you."

Storm snorted, "So he said. He said a lot of words. Slut, I recall, was one of them"

"He thought, if I hit on you, it would make you uncomfortable and you'd leave. I told him I did and he didn't understand why it didn't work, why you're still here and not acting particularly upset. He was thinking about it too hard, so I told him you kind of acted like you didn't mind so much. I said maybe your marriage was going to hell and you were looking for someone to give you some attention."

"Jesus, and he fell for that?" she asked, turning to look up at him.

Martin lifted a strand of hair from her face, tucked it carefully behind her ear and then let his forearm rest lightly on her shoulder. It was almost an embrace.

"He seemed to fall for it. Said something about my Latin charm. In any case be good if you played along, at least try to pretend I don't repulse you."

"I'll try. It won't be easy."

"I know," Martin said, with a smile that sparkled in his dark eyes.

Flustered and suddenly unnerved, Storm stepped back. Martin removed his arm, reached past and opened the door for her.

"Guess I'll help Mom, uh Lisa, with some housework or something," she said.

Back inside, Storm did look for her mother, but not with the intention of helping her with housework. She found her sitting on a tall stool at the kitchen island, a newspaper spread out in front of her, a cup of untouched coffee nearby.

Lisa looked up when Storm entered the room. "I hate politics," she said, turning the page and smoothing it with her palm.

"Don't we all," said Storm. Someone was playing on the piano in the main room. It was an old song, The Blue Danube Waltz. Storm recognized it because she'd taken piano for a short time and it was one of those iconic first songs they always taught you.

"It's Jackie. I've been giving her lessons, sort of." Lisa smiled sheepishly, as if at the audacity that she could teach someone.

Storm had forgotten that her mother played piano, or that she'd been the one who signed Storm up for piano classes that they couldn't really afford. A cost that had led to one of her parent's epic fights.

"At least she's keeping them entertained," said Storm. Lowering her voice, she asked, "Do you have a computer?"

Lisa furrowed her brow at the unexpected request. "Well sure, a laptop."

"Where is it?"

"In my bedroom. Why? Do you want to borrow it?"

"Yes, but I don't want them to know it. Can you come up with a reason we both need to go upstairs and spend some time?"

"We could go up and check on Joe."

"I'd rather keep him out of this."

Lisa thought about it for a moment, took a sip of her coffee, made a face and set it down. "We agreed we wouldn't contact the police. It's too dangerous."

"That's not what I want it for. I promise."

Lisa thought about it a moment then said, "The rooms need a good cleaning. Want to help?"

"No," said Storm, more loudly this time. "But I will."

Lisa got up, and Storm followed her to the closet that held the washer and dryer as well as cleaning supplies. Lisa grabbed an empty bucket, tossed in some cleaning cloths, handed Storm a spray bottle of all-surface cleaner and they headed upstairs to work.

Bud walked into the kitchen as if he expected to catch them up to something. "What are you ladies doing?" he asked. Nonchalantly reaching for the coffee pot.

Storm realized her instinct was right. From now on they'd need an excuse for everything they did. The men were watching them more closely. Something was about to happen. The tension was growing.

"Going upstairs to tidy up," said Lisa. "Might as well put my daughter to work while I've got her around, right?" she said, smiling as if Bud would appreciate the joke.

When they reached the landing Storm noticed her bedroom door was open. She peeked in to find her father fast asleep on top of the covers. He'd propped his knee on a couple of pillows and the bag of ice had fallen aside, a small wet area on the quilt showed where the bag had leaked. Storm held her index finger to her lips and they tiptoed past.

The next room was a bathroom. Lisa instructed Storm to take all the little knickknacks, roll up the small throw rugs and put them in the hall, while she sprayed the walls of the bathtub and the rest of the fixtures. They moved carefully so as not to make too much noise and wake Joe.

"We'll let that sit for a while, while we hit the bathroom on the other side. The folks downstairs can use the half bath for now."

Storm thought Lisa sounded like someone talking to a new employee. She guessed it was a more familiar role than mother. That was probably sad, she decided, but she also found it amusing.

They walked past the other rooms, and around the narrow end to the other side of the landing. Here, the bathroom was the first room. They performed the same actions, then Lisa checked the entry area and seeing no one, quickly moved to the last room in the row. Taking a key from her pocket, she unlocked the door and they went in.

Storm noticed the room was twice the size of hers and overlooked the north side of the lodge and the road winding in from town. Aware of the need to hurry, Storm nonetheless couldn't help but take a few seconds to scrutinize the space that was her mother's personal refuge.

In contrast to the rest of the lodge, with its overstuffed and homey collections, the room was uncluttered though not without character. The colors were blue and white, with dark navy curtains held back with thick white rope, a white bedspread, a blue and white braided rug with flecks of red woven throughout.

A framed painting of a stormy sea and a trio of ships tossed on the waves took up most of one wall. Aside from that, the only decorations were a giant seashell and couple of framed photographs, one of

Storm and one of her with Tom and the kids, atop a squat white dresser. Beneath the window an old maple desk with built in file cabinets held a laptop and a tiffany-style lamp as well as a scattering of documents that looked like bills and junk mail.

Storm went directly to the computer, flipped up its lid and pressed the on button. It seemed to take forever for the login screen to appear, but Storm knew that it had only been seconds.

"Sorry," she said to her mother, apologizing for her lack of manners in handling her property without taking the time to ask. "Is it password protected?"

Lisa nodded. "It's lindseyjoel, no break, all lower case."

Hearing her children's names made Storm pause, but she recovered and typed the password then hit enter.

The desktop popped up and Storm searched the edge of the machine for a USB port. She found an empty one and inserted the flash drive.

"What is that?" her mother whispered.

"Joe and I found it, and a lot more just like it, in a box. It's what they were so freaked out about. I need to see what's on it."

Though a chair stood in front of the desk both women ignored it and leaned forward, eager to learn what the LOC were going to so much trouble to transport.

There was no sound, no intro, only a sudden flash of color and motion. The unsteady hand of a camera operator adjusting the focus brought into clarity a scene that Storm had not expected. It took her a moment to make out that what she was seeing was a man's straining buttocks and thighs as he moved back and forth in a rhythm as old as time.

Pornography. That's what it was all about. Storm was filled with disgust, and as the man turned, looked over his shoulder and grinned, a shudder rolled down her spine. She had never expected to see a familiar face. It was Leon, his face sweating with exertion, the tip of his tongue protruding between his lips. With a wink and a smirk, he pushed himself to his feet and stood to the side, revealing his partner.

Storm heard her mother's gasp. A young girl lay there panting for air. The tiny child had been trapped beneath the weight of the adult above her, obviously barely able to breathe. Thin arms pushed against the mattress as she scuttled away from the man, or the camera, or both. No more than eleven or twelve, Storm guessed, the girl's fine blond hair was matted, her face wet with sweat and snot. A smear of blood was bright against the pale skin of her thighs until she dragged herself to the head of the bed, were she drew her legs up and curled into herself, much as Marty had. Storm saw a pattern of bruises, the kind that would be made by a man's strong fingers, on the girl's hips.

Leon's hand came back into the frame as he playfully swatted the girl's behind. She didn't move, but Leon's smirk grew into a smile. Storm thought the emotion on his face was pride. A sort of low level pride, the kind he might wear after winning a hand of black jack or a game of darts.

She clicked the stop button and froze the picture. Leon's face filled the center of the frame, the girl in the far-left corner. On the monitor screen Storm caught a glimpse of her own face, her eyes glittering with rage, her lips pulled back from her teeth.

She shook it off; the appearance of rage, the emotion of anger. She pushed it down, deep into the well she had built so many years ago. But she did not place the cover over it, as she normally did, a symbolic way of keeping her negative emotions suppressed. This time she left the emotions contained but accessible. Needing only for her to call on their dark essence to power what she would do next.

"Mom," she said, addressing her mother with the term purposefully for the first time. "Don't worry. That son-of-a-bitch will pay." The room seemed to grow darker under the weight of the promise contained in those words.

"What are you going to do?" Lisa asked, her voice trembling from shock at what she'd seen or possibly from something she saw on Storm's face.

Storm didn't know, or particularly care. She only noted it as a fact, as she'd noted the furniture in the room, the colors, the textures.

"Right now, I'm going to finish what we started and clean those bathrooms."

Lisa nodded, and though she looked as if she wanted to say something more, she didn't.

Storm took the flash drive out of the laptop and held it on her palm. "We need to find a safe place to hide this."

Lisa stared at it, a look of complete disgust on her face, silent and unmoving.

"Mom," Storm said.

Hearing the word mom broke the spell of inaction that had fallen over Lisa. "I have an idea, give it to me," Lisa said.

Storm held out her hand and her mother reached out and took the flashdrive between her thumb and forefinger, touching it as little as possible.

Storm watched as Lisa took a scissor from a cup on her desk, went to the curtains and pulled them up, cut a strand of thread and dropped the flash drive through the opening and into the hem. When she let it go it hung just as it had before. "We should probably hurry," she suggested.

They went back to the bathroom nearest Storm's room and began scrubbing. "That little girl, she was barely older than Lindsey," Lisa whispered.

"I know," said Storm, realizing how traumatizing this would be for her mother, but also aware this wasn't the time to try and deal with it.

The girls age being close to Lindsey's had been her first thought, her second thought had been, how am I going to kill Leon?

I understand you need someone to talk to about what we just saw. I've been there and I get it, but now is not the time. If someone comes up here I don't want them to hear us talking. Let's finish cleaning in silence while I concentrate on a plan. All I want them to see is a couple of mousy woman overly concerned with making them comfortable.

Lisa's lips twisted at the word mousy, but she nodded, and turned back to wiping the mirror above the sink.

Storm heard footsteps on the stairs ignored them and kept working. As Bud moved into view, poking his head into the bathroom, Storm felt grateful that they'd made it back before he got there, and that they hadn't been talking. She was more certain than ever that they were keeping an eye on them. It looked like for now it was Bud's turn to play watchdog.

"About done in there?"

"Downstairs bathroom not working?" Lisa asked. Storm felt a moment of concern at the snappy tone of her mother's voice. This was no time to provoke them, but she understood her mother's anger all too well. Luckily Bud didn't seem to notice.

"Occupied," Bud said.

"We're almost done. There," Storm said, taking a final swipe at the mirror. "It's all yours. Without another word she took her mother's arm and gently but firmly pushed her out of the room and down the hallway.

They were working on the second bathroom when Joe appeared at the doorway.

"I see you're awake," said Lisa.

"I can't even believe I fell asleep in the middle of the day. Must be old age."

"Or busted ribs," said Storm.

"Feeling better?" Lisa asked. "How's the knee?"

He looked down at his knee. Lisa caught Storm's eye. Storm could sense the unasked question, should we tell your father? She shook her head. Before involving him in her plan she needed to talk to Martin and learn if the FBI was really planning to bury Leon and everyone involved in the deepest pit they could find.

If so, she was willing to stand back and wait for justice to do its thing. She realized that she could kill

Leon, but that might allow the rest of them to escape justice.

However, if Leon was just a small fish in a pond full of big fish, someone who would be forgiven in exchange for a shot at a more valuable player, then his future would turn out very differently.

But knowing herself she was fairly sure that, no matter what the FBI had planned, from the moment she'd seen that video, Leon's future had been decided.

Her gun was gone. They'd taken it. But as she stood there, looking at her father, she thought about the duffel bag in the closet and the pleasant weight of the knife she'd found inside. The memory made her smile.

CHAPTER FIFTEEN

ON SATURDAY, Storm woke and pushed her blankets off. She looked toward the cot but her father was already up and out. Stretching until she heard her shoulders pop she yawned then just laid there. A bar of sunlight lay diagonally across her, she could feel it's heat on her forearms and across her thighs. It was going to be a hot day, or so she hoped.

She wondered what had awakened her, then decided it was a combination of the heat and the retreating popcorn popper sound of a motorcycle's exhaust. She sat up, her dark hair sliding into her face. She pushed it back and tucked it behind her ears.

The motion reminded her of Martin, of his fingers sliding behind her ear as he put a stray strand away. Was she attracted to the man? That was a stupid question. Obviously she was. He was not just good-looking, he was also a man seeking justice. They had that in common, even if their methods were different.

She thought of Tom then. Remembered him chasing Joel, their youngest, through the house. Joel shrieking as he ran, not too fast, to get away from the tickle monster. Thought of Tom's slightly balding but nicely shaped head. The worry lines around his eyes. The laugh lines around his mouth. Thought of his eyes, and how he looked as he held his weight and lowered himself to her. Remembered that he was the one she had always loved. The first person she'd ever let herself care for and the unbelievable luck of finding he felt the same about her.

The memories brought a certain heat and unwanted thoughts of tongues and hips and sweat slick skin. Tom's tongue. Tom's hands. Almost of its own volition her hand slid down her stomach, under the waistband of her pants, tight around her wrist, and came to rest, her fingertips just parting the skin above her swelling . . .

"No." She said the word as softly as breathing. Slid her hand free. Leon's leering face had popped into her thoughts and destroyed every hint of heat.

She got up and began gathering her clothes and her thoughts. The clothes were simple. The thoughts a bit more complicated. By the time she'd assembled her things she'd come to two comforting conclusions. One, Leon would pay. Two, Martin was exciting, but it was Tom she had been thinking of in the heat of the moment. It was Tom she wanted.

Showered and dressed, Storm returned to her room, ostensibly to put her dirty laundry away, but once she'd done that she found herself kneeling before her father's duffle bag, which sat on the floor just inside the closet. She felt around until she found the knife, still rolled in an old shirt.

It was a very large knife. Some sort of military issue, she thought. Maybe, if it had a sheath, she could have hidden it, put it down the back of her pants maybe, with a tight belt to keep it in place. But it had no sheath and the edge was so sharp that when she touched it lightly with her thumb to test it she'd cut herself. She put it back where she'd found it with some regret.

Her frustration over the lack of a gun or a knife was rather ironic considering one of her rules had always been to avoid weapons. A dog leash could work as easily as a noose and never attract the same kind of attention. A baseball bat was as good a club as any. Even the innocent knitting needles stuck through a ball of pink yarn, when applied properly, could be lethal.

She and her first partner, Howard, had killed in many ways, often with just the strength of his hands. With Lauren it had been different. Lacking a man's strength, they'd been forced to find alternatives. Yet here she was, ready to cry over the lack of a weapon. *Pathetic*, she told herself.

The waiting was starting to get to her. Martin's guess, that the meeting was going to take place soon hadn't helped. Not having a phone was also making her a little crazy. The idea of sneaking out to a nearby farm to borrow a phone to call Tom kept creeping into her thoughts. It was ridiculous, the cost of hearing Tom's voice would be too high. She'd be putting her family at risk.

She reached the kitchen to find Martin sitting in the breakfast nook, rolling a cup of coffee between his hands, a plate of bacon and eggs congealing in front of him.

"I thought I'd find my mother in here," she said, as she crossed the kitchen and took a coffee cup from the tray.

"They're out in the garden doing something, pulling weeds maybe."

"Where's everyone else?"

"Your father went for a walk, said he needed to stretch out his knee. Leon and Bud are heading to town. Perro is out messing with the dogs, giving them a bath or something."

"How does he manage that?" she asked, remembering the dog's barred teeth and low growls in the presence of their sadistic owner.

"Feeds them doggie valium until they quit trying to rip him to pieces. I expect one of these days they'll fool him and he'll get his throat torn out."

"I'd pay for seats," said Storm, without sarcasm.

She took her coffee and leaned against the island, facing him.

"I gather you're on guard duty today. Keeping an eye on us while the rest are out. That's good because we need to talk," she told him.

"Your mother left you a plate of food in the fridge."

"That was nice, but I'm not hungry."

"She's a nice lady," he said.

"I'm starting to realize that."

"Your dad's not too bad either."

Storm shrugged. "We need to talk."

"What about?"

"I know what your biker friends are selling. Do you?"

"How'd you manage that?" His eyes widened. "Oh, don't tell me. When your dad took the box. You guys did find a computer in the woods."

"More or less."

"Not smart."

"Information is the definition of smart," she said, disagreeing.

"Tell me what you know."

"I know why you're FBI and not ATF."

"Tell me."

"You want to go for another walk?"

"I just want you to tell me what you know."

Storm found she was enjoying herself a bit too much, but that didn't stop her.

"Marty needs his breakfast."

"I need to . . . Fine, we'll go feed the damn dog."

"Good." Storm found a plastic container and shoveled Martin's uneaten breakfast into it, then went to the fridge to find what Lisa had left for her. She added the cold bacon and scrambled eggs to the container. The sight of the food made her slightly nauseous, or maybe it was the growing tension at work on her stomach.

Marty stood when she opened the car door, and though his tail and ears were down Storm felt encouraged that she was beginning to gain his trust. She set the bowl down, then stepped back so he could eat in peace, which he did, wolfing the food down and licking the container until it fell to the floor.

Feeling the growing impatience of Martin behind her, Storm reached in and snapped the chain to his namesake's collar. As soon as Marty jumped from the car he tugged her in the direction of the road, following the path she and Martin had taken with him before.

"Smart dog," Martin noted, seeing where he was headed.

Storm said, "He is, but we have to be smarter. Let's stay out of Perro's sight." She encouraged Marty to move farther north of the house and waited while a white pickup with a double rack of kayaks drove by.

Unlike the last time, this time when they reached the cool shadows cast by the trees, it came as a relief. Neither of them spoke until they reached the clearing and the view of the lake opened below them, the hot sun making silver spoons across the surface of the lake.

"Kiddie porn," Storm said, her eyes locked on the lake.

"What do you want to know?" Martin asked.

"Tell me when and for how long you plan to lock that animal and his friends away? I know you want the boss. I get that but tell me Leon is going to pay."

"You watched the flash drive. Can you tell me what you saw?"

"Leon. A little girl. Evil."

"Leon. We didn't know that."

Storm turned toward him, saw the shocked expression he wore and believed him.

"You really didn't know?"

"We knew he, they, were transporting. We thought maybe trafficking as well. That's why we got called in. We're part of a joint task force, the DOJ, FBI. You okay?"

Storm realized she was shaking. She took a deep breath. Took another breath. "No, not okay." She didn't tell him that she felt like her skin was on fire, that the intensity of the heat had nothing to do with the warmth of the day. That the sensation was so bad that she was afraid to look down at herself, afraid she might actually be burning, her flesh white hot, melting. She tightened her grip on Marty's chain until the links dug into the skin of her palm. The pain made her feel a little better, took her out of the downward spiral of her thoughts.

"What can I do to help?" Martin asked, his voice soft with concern.

"Let's keep walking."

Marty was tugging at the leash and she followed him, letting the untrained animal pull her along at his pace. Martin walked beside her. Moving helped.

"Talk to me, tell me what you know about Leon and the others," she said as the emotions that had momentarily overwhelmed her slowly abated.

"Leon," he began, "Leon Lee Ray, thirty-two years old. Two years ago he came to our attention because his cousin Brandon Ray, also called Blade, was charged with production of child pornography. He'd been online using this site known for child porn. Our guys got a search warrant, tracked him to his house, confiscated his computer and found images of a girl, about nine, tied up naked on his bed. They suspected he'd paid for the girl and had her shipped over from Thailand, but we couldn't prove it and we haven't found her. Best we could do was get him on production of sexually explicit images of a minor and have him sent to Pelican Bay.

"That bust put us onto Leon. When we checked his computer it also had a ton of porn. Initially, he said the images just popped up and he'd delete them, but then it got to be too much trouble. It wasn't a good story, especially when they found over a hundred images and videos of juveniles in sex acts. That's when he claimed they weren't his, that his cousin had borrowed his computer and must have loaded them. Sadly, the judge only gave him a slap on the wrist.

"I had been working another case, part of a DOJ initiative called Project Protect the Children to fight child abuse and sexual exploitation. I got close to someone in the organization and was invited to go to church, which is lingo for a motorcycle club meeting. The club was the LOC and Leon was appointed interim leader until Blade was able to work out a way to run things from prison.

"Since then I've been working on earning my patch. Until I do, I won't have their full trust. Perro is the new guy so he's taking some of the heat that used to be on me. They aren't even letting him ride a bike until he shows them he can handle one properly. In the meanwhile, they're making him drive the pickup and deal with the dogs. We're pretty sure the truck is a transport vehicle for the porn and the dogs are to keep people away. Perro's supposed to keep them vicious and he's certainly taken to the job. Came close to shooting the little psycho myself."

"I told you," Storm reminded him. "I didn't shoot Perro."

"Sure, I know," said Martin, his tone belying his words.

"Anyway, I thought biker gangs were all about drugs," said Storm.

"Not biker gangs," Martin corrected her, "Motorcycle clubs, that's what they prefer."

"Fuck what they prefer," Storm snapped. "What about the drugs?"

"You're right, a lot of motorcycle clubs depend on drug sales or gun running but if you've read the news you've probably heard about the drug cartels in Mexico."

"Sure."

"Well, their guys are a little more hard-assed than a lot of our guys. Lots of the bikers now are less in the business of running a drug transport and more in the business of working for a cartel that runs a drug transport. Not everyone likes being second or third dog.

"Besides, as far as the LOC goes, their leader was probably already a pedophile. From what you tell me, so is his cousin. Don't want to think about what their family life was like. Anyway, Blade probably dropped some serious money on his hobby, so he knew how to hook things up when they decided to go that way to make money. I figure since they had to pay for it, and someone was going to make it, it might as well be them."

"So, that's the route, go from watching porn to making porn, to selling porn."

"Just like drugs. Same trajectory," said Martin.

Storm realized she was thirsty, and wished she'd brought a bottle of water with her. As if reading her mind, Martin said, "We should get back. I don't know where your father went and as you guessed, I'm supposed to be keeping an eye on him. On all of you, actually.

"I know it took him awhile to cut off your lines of communication and disable your cars but he's not an idiot. He knows you could take a short walk and borrow a neighbor's phone, call the cops, blow up this meeting. He's getting more and more twitchy and I have no idea what Blades' going to suggest he do to handle you and your family. Stealing the box, that was not a good thing to do. Worse to get caught. I'm hoping he won't tell Blade about you and your father showing up. Be the smart thing to do. Guy's gotta look good, look smart, or he'll lose his place. Might be the best for all of you."

"I thought you could protect us."

"Not if you never do what I ask you to do."

"Well, there's that." Tugging on Marty's leash she got him turned back onto the path and they started back the way they'd come.

Martin smiled, but it didn't reach his eyes. "Did you put the flash drive back in the box?"

"Of course."

"Good. If they count them, and the count's off there'll be hell to pay."

"You could lose your patch."

This time Martin really did smile, "Haven't earned it yet."

"I have confidence in you."

"We'll get them, you know," he said, suddenly serious.

"I hope so."

"It must have been hard to see whatever you saw on the flash drive."

"It was . . . It was bad," Storm agreed. The image of Leon and the girl flashed through her mind. She tried to shy away from it. The memory of Leon's face stoked her anger into a blaze, the image of the girl turned it into an inferno. She was barely able to contain herself and stop from marching back to the house, retrieving her father's knife and stabbing Leon through his vile heart.

"It's one of the hardest things there is for someone investigating this sort of crime," he was saying. "Watching hours and hours of this filth can make you crazy, give you PTSD. Our agents have to get counseling, do all sorts of things to get those images out of their heads."

"What do you do?" Storm asked.

Martin gave her a bemused smile, looked around at the trees and the lake, "Go for long walks. I try to focus on something else, pretend they're just a bad movie and not real and sometimes . . . sometimes I imagine cutting small pieces out of those guys, little cubes of flesh. Ahhh, see?" he told her. "Can't think about this stuff too much."

Storm nodded, understanding more than he knew. The faces of the victims that had driven her to become a vigilante were always there, waiting for her to think of them, to bring back their precious faces. To see again those eyes that should have held nothing more than youthful exuberance, but reflected instead only cynicism, pain and fear.

"I think we should tell my family who you are," Storm suggested.

"No. You can't," Martin said forcefully.

"But they're scared. I'm scared too, but at least I know you're here and that you can call in help if you need it. That helps. It would help them too."

"That's the problem. They'd be less scared, and Leon would sense that, he's very good at sensing those sorts of things. The minute he suspects I'm a cop is the minute I'm dead and the rest of you are in serious trouble."

"And we're not in trouble now?"

"No, because the last thing Leon wants is drama. He wants this meeting to go well so he can report to the boss that his network will continue, is continuing. Then he'll hand Leon vital information which we can use to find that network and take it down. Isn't that what you want?"

Storm nodded. "That and Leon. I want to know, whatever else happens, Leon pays."

"He'll pay. I promise."

Storm looked into Martin's dark brown eyes and saw what she hoped was the truth.

"Okay," she said, "I'll hold you to it."

CHAPTER
SIXTEEN

STORM WAS RELIEVED to see her father had returned to the house and was sitting on the top step of the front stairs. That relief turned to irritation when she realized he was waiting for her, a displeased look on his face. She stood at the bottom of the stairs, planning to take Marty back to her car, as Martin took the stairs two at a time. Her father ignored him as he went past and into the house.

When the front door closed, Joe said, "What did he want? Why does he follow you every time you go for a walk? Doesn't he think you can walk that dog by yourself?"

Storm reached down and patted the dog in question. Marty had stopped beside her, and at the tone of her father's voice was pressing against her leg. She could feel the light tremble through her pants and realized that the dog was either anxious or angry. She didn't want to see the result of either.

"It's okay," she told the dog in a soothing tone. "Not sure which of your questions to answer first." she said in the same calm voice to her father. "Maybe he just likes to walk. Maybe he's just a harmless flirt."

"Nothing harmless about him, or those other men," Joe said. "You understand what a motorcycle club is, what it expects from its members? I'll tell you," he said, without waiting for a response. "Loyalty. Doesn't sound like much, does it, but it means everything to them. In the name of loyalty they'll do anything for each other, cheat, lie, steal, worse. It's the thing that drives them to join and to stay. That allegiance to something gives them purpose, and the more loyal they are the more they're rewarded. No matter what he tells you, he'll always put the men in his club ahead of you."

"You sound like you think I'm going to leave my husband and kids and run away with him," Storm said, not sure whether to be amused or angry.

"Oh, good heavens no." He started to stand but then sat back down, his face flushed red to the tips of his ears. "I never meant to imply any such thing. I was just trying to explain to you that every sweet word he whispers is a lie."

"I get that. Trust me, the only reason I let him talk to me at all is I'm hoping he'll give me some information. Something that will get them to leave Lisa alone."

"There's one sure way to get them to leave her alone."

"What's that?"

"Take away what they have on your mother and let her fight back, call the cops, do whatever it takes. All she needs to know is that what they think they have on you is a lie. Just find a way to prove it to her."

Somewhere a tree frog made a thin piping sound, and from the lake, the distant sound of a motorboat, but there, on the front steps of the lodge there was only a profound silence.

Joe's gaze was too much for Storm to hold. She stared down at Marty, calmer now, and stretched out, but with his ears raised, one cocked forward, the other toward her.

Storm watched Joe struggle with his growing realization of what her silence might mean. Finally he said, "So, they were right. Lauren Barry, that poor woman I hurt, that woman in the mental hospital . . . you're saying she told the truth?"

She looked up and this time met his eyes. She had almost wavered, ready to make a full confession, to let him carry some of the burden of her guilt. But that was selfish and stupid. So, she didn't confess. Instead, drawing on her best acting skills she ignored his question and sighed, as if her moment of silence was one of reflection on his accusation, rather than a form of admission. "There are people in this world who are not meant to live. You've been in prison. Surely, you met pure evil in there."

Joe rubbed his hands together as if they were cold, clasping and unclasping his fingers nervously. He took his time, considering the question. "Yes. Yes, I have. There are a lot of terrible people in this world and I did get to know some of them while inside."

"Do you honestly believe I'm one of them? That I'm capable of doing what this woman said?"

"No. No." Joe said, looking very uncomfortable. Storm could tell he was beginning to backpedal. "You don't seem like that."

"No, and I'm not, but I forgive you for thinking I could be. You don't know me. But I do know that woman in the mental institution and she is pure unadulterated evil. You can believe that. Someday, when this is all over, if you want to hear about it, I'll be happy to tell you the whole story."

Joe avoided looking at Storm. Instead his head hung down in much the same way her son Joel's did after a rare scolding. She felt guilty for lying but the truth would not be better for him. That much she knew for sure.

"I'm sorry," he said softly, and met her eyes reluctantly before again looking away.

After a few awkward moments of silence, he got to his feet somewhat unsteadily. She saw he used the stair rail to help himself up. Was it his knee, his ribs or something else making him unsteady. Had he believed her and felt guilty for having considered, even for a moment, that his daughter could be a killer?

"I have to get some ice for this knee . . . we'll talk later," he said, and made his way slowly across the porch.

Unsettled, Storm took Marty to the car. She undid his leash and gestured and the dog jumped in as if he'd done it his whole life. Storm glanced at the pickup but Perro was no longer inside. She looked toward the dogs but they were also out of sight. Having no reason to hurry into the lodge, she slid into the back seat of her car.

"Good dog," she said to Marty. "Good boy."

Marty picked up one of the pieces of the rubber ball she'd given him earlier and began to chew on it, dropping it now and then, just to trap it under a paw before grabbing it again.

"Part cat aren't you," she said, as she unconsciously stroked the torn ears and fell into thought about her parents. If her father got this upset about the possibility that Lauren was telling the truth, how was her mother taking it so calmly? After all, she had to believe Storm was a vigilante, otherwise the LOC would have nothing to use on her.

"My mother thinks I'm a killer, but she's still trying to protect me," she told Marty. "My father," he's not sure what he thinks."

Why did her mother believe them? Storm pondered. Did she see something in me when I was a kid? Did she know the early signs of a killer? Storm knew them. It was Serial Killer 101.

"Killers tend to have some things in common," she told Marty. "First, they often like to start fires. I don't remember ever setting a fire. In fact, ever since Joe set me on fire, I've kind of had an aversion to them." She chuckled softly. Marty continued gnawing on his toy.

"Two, they like to torture animals. Well, we know that's not me. Now Perro, we may have to look at him.

"Three, they drink or do drugs. Nope. Can't stand the taste or the weird way it makes you feel. No control? No way.

"Four, they fantasize about killing. I'm not totally sure about that one," she told Marty. "I don't think planning justice killings count, that's logistics not fantasizing, right?"

Marty didn't respond so she went on.

"Five, a messed-up, abusive family life. Well sure, but who didn't have one of those? That shouldn't even count, right Marty?"

Leaning back in her seat she patted Marty while she wondered again. What was it that led her mother to believe what Leon told her? More importantly, had Tom seen it too? Had he ever suspected that his wife was late because she was out stalking and killing? He was much closer to her than her mother, so if she saw signs surely so had he. Maybe he just kept his suspicions to himself because he, like she, didn't want to ruin their perfect illusion of a happy family.

She closed her eyes, felt the pulse of something darker than blood flowing through her veins. Not a perfect family, a perfect daddy and two perfect kids maybe, but the core was rotten, the mommy was a monster and the stain of that would touch all of them eventually.

"Fuck you, Joe," she said, her eyes flashing open but seeing only the face of her father. She heard the click of the lighter, smelled the rum, and relived, in the confines of the backseat, the moment she was transformed from fearful child to remorseless monster.

Marty whined and tried to climb onto her lap. His long nails dug into her thigh and the sharp pain drove the unhappy memory from her mind. She pushed him away, gently but firmly, then slid her hands along his muzzle and looked deep into his eyes. "I'm good, it's okay," she told him. She found another section of his favorite toy on the floor of the car and teased him with it until it took his full attention.

"Well, even monsters have their uses, right?" she asked Marty. Then she got out of the car.

CHAPTER SEVENTEEN

TOO WOUND UP to sit still, Storm went into the garden where she found her mother digging up weeds with a garden hoe.

"Where's Jackie?" she asked.

"Jackie's in her room," Lisa said, slamming the hoe into the ground hard. "Says she has a headache." Again she dug the tool into the dirt. "We both know her only headache is a hangover, don't we?"

Storm nodded her agreement.

"Your father's up in his room icing his knee again. Looks like the help is falling apart," her mother quipped.

"What can I help you with out here?"

"Well, I didn't mean to imply that I needed your help," Lisa said, "but since you're asking," She stopped digging, looked around and said, "I could use your help with everything. The weeds are getting out of hand. The fence needs to be tightened where the deer have been pushing against it. There's a broken board that needs to be replaced." She waved her hand toward a raised bed with wooden sides.

Storm went to the end of a row of onions and knelt. The ground was damp and muddy and Lisa asked if she'd like a pad to kneel on and some gloves but Storm said no. She loved to garden and knew that those things would only serve to separate her from the full experience. She found the smell of the earth and the grass soothing. Even the sting of the tiny cuts in the palms of her gloveless hands was a welcome distraction from her thoughts.

Methodically she pulled and dug until her hands and nails were filthy and a small ache in her shoulders reminded her she hadn't done this kind of work in a while. As she finished the first row and moved on to the next she realized she was humming under her breath. It was a strange sensation for her to be so relaxed, and the moment she realized it her normal state of hyper awareness kicked in and her senses came alive.

She could hear her mother's hammer as she worked replacing the broken side of the raised bed. Moments ago, nails screeched as they reluctantly gave up their hold on the old board as Lisa pried it loose. The sound had drawn Joe, but seeing his obvious limp, both women had waved him back into the house and to the book he'd been reading.

Martin was inside with Perro. When she'd last seen them Martin was playing solitaire, while Perro looked on and made suggestions from the side lines. With the forceful personality of Leon and the off color humor of Bud gone, Storm thought the house seemed calmer. Martin and Perro could have been a couple of guys having a lazy day off.

Such moments were always short, in Storm's experience. As soon as she had the thought she caught the sound of motorcycles at the edge of her perception.

"Damn."

"What?" asked Lisa.

"They're coming back. I can hear their bikes."

"Damn," Lisa said, echoing her daughter. Then she turned back to the task at hand.

Not knowing what else to do, Storm did the same, though it was hard to pretend nothing had changed. The entire atmosphere was suddenly charged and

Storm's concentration was now directed at listening for the men to enter the house. So keen was her focus that she actually heard the front door open before hearing the bell. There were muffled words between the men that she couldn't make out.

As she got to her feet, preparing to carry a bucket of weeds to the compost pile, she heard the distinct sound of tires on gravel. Had she heard a car coming up the road? She wasn't sure, but she certainly heard one pulling into the driveway.

Storm looked at Lisa. She had set down her hammer and was taking off her gloves, preparing to meet whoever had arrived.

"Did you hear a car pull in?" Storm asked.

"Yes, I think so," said Lisa. "I bet Jackie's still in her room, or Bud's so I better run in and see who's here."

Storm wondered who it could be. A guest? A delivery? Him? There was no reason to worry yet, but her sense of dread was unmistakable. Once again, Storm heard the front door open before the sound of the bell.

She dumped the bucket of weeds, set it down and rubbed her hands together to remove some of the mud. Before her mom reached the door, it flew open, causing both of them to jump.

Leon glared at the two women. "You gals need to hustle. We've got company and I promised them lunch."

"You got it," Lisa said.

"Screw you," Storm said under her breath, so quietly only she could hear it.

Leon nodded and went back inside.

Lisa turned to Storm and smiled, "Now, now, is that any way to treat a guest?"

Apparently she hadn't spoken as quietly as she thought.

"I couldn't help myself," Storm said, smiling ear to ear.

As they entered they saw Leon with a man Storm hadn't seen before. He was tall, well built, and handsome enough to model expensive suits or watches. He wore one of those on his wrist, a thick gold thing that screamed money. He also wore jeans and a burgundy polo shirt that tried to seem casual but somehow failed. Champagne clung to the stranger's arm like a parasitic but shapely bug.

He looked down at the mud-spattered women and sneered. The obvious arrogance of the man irritated Storm. She could feel her resentment growing and he hadn't said a word.

"These are the people who are going to make lunch?" he asked Leon. "I hope they plan to wash their hands first."

Leon laughed as if he'd just heard the best joke ever.

Storm's lips twisted. If she didn't already hate this messenger of Blade's she would quickly learn to.

"We didn't think you'd be here until dinner but I'm sure we can find something you'll like," Lisa said in a pleasant tone, as if she were addressing normal guests.

"Sounds good," said Leon.

Martin, Bud and Perro came from the kitchen, Perro carrying two six packs. With the arrival of the beer they all went out back.

In the kitchen, Storm and Lisa washed their hands.

"I guess the meeting is about to start," said Storm.

"Looks like it. Why do you think he's here?" asked Lisa.

"I think he's here to give orders to the men from their boss at Pelican Bay."

"Where did you get that idea?" Lisa asked.

For a moment, Storm's blood ran cold. The answer was: from Martin. Without what she hoped was too much hesitation she said, "I heard them talking." She was amazed at her ability to lie so easily, but then, perhaps it was genetic.

"You really think their boss is in Pelican Bay?"

"Yes. I overheard them talking about it. I think that man works at the prison and passes messages from their boss to the club."

"That's terrible. I wonder what he does at the prison?"

"Don't know. Could be a guard, a cook, maybe a pharmacist, therapist, or hell, even a priest. Could be anyone."

"Well, I sure don't think that's a man of God," said Lisa. "Not the way Champagne was hanging all over him. Speaking of which, did you notice the way Leon didn't even seem to care? I thought she was his girlfriend."

"I have the impression Leon likes his women younger," said Storm.

At this, Lisa recoiled.

Storm immediately regretted what she'd said. She too couldn't help but remember the horrific scene she'd witnessed."

"Yes, and I imagine Champagne is the kind of woman who is easily interchangeable for another," said Lisa, clearly trying to change the subject.

"If that's true, it's sad."

"I guess so," said Lisa. Is this the only kind of men Champagne can see herself with? If so you have to wonder why. Could she have been traumatized at a young age? If that's the case, do we have any right to judge her?"

"Oh, I don't have any problems judging her," said Storm, as she grabbed a steak knife and began cutting pickles into slices to go with the cold cuts.

Ignoring Storm's comment, her mother pulled open a drawer, reached inside, grabbed a paring knife and handed it to her. "Here, use this, it's sharper. We need tomato slices too. They're in the crisper."

Storm finished with the pickles and started on the tomatoes, placing the slices on a plate alongside the pickles, to go with the trays of cold cuts and cheeses her mother was uncovering. Feeling as if she needed to explain her earlier comment about judging Champagne, Storm said, "I made peace with judging people a long time ago, when I decided to take the job with probation and parole. Laws aren't perfect, and one size doesn't fit all, but design a society without them and it all turns to chaos."

"I guess my outlook is a little more liberal than that," Lisa replied, "I hope someday we can talk about it in more depth. Right now the only thing I can focus on is if those men really plan to leave after this meeting, and if they'll be coming back."

Storm nodded, but thought. And all I can think about is how to get a gun and make sure they don't go anywhere after this meeting. Once again, the horrific image of Leon and the young girl flashed through her thoughts. As she filled a tray with two choices of bread her hands shook.

Storm and her mother carried the trays outside and set them on the table. The weather was perfect for lunch outdoors. It had warmed up but there was a soft breeze and the sun, though bright, was hidden much of the time by a scattering of clouds that promised evening showers.

Birds flitted through the trees at the top of the hillside, chirping and singing and calling to each other. Butterflies swooped around the garden, adding colorful notes to the lush green. The day was so idyllic Storm couldn't help thinking about Tom and the kids and how much they'd love it at the lodge. She could imagine Tom sitting at the table, face to the sun, eyes closed. She could see the kids playing in the garden, picking peas and sneaking strawberries.

"Thought we agreed Joe would be the waiter," Martin said.

"We forgot," said Storm. "His knee's still bothering him. He's laying down."

"I'm so used to running the lodge I didn't even think," said Lisa.

"Yeah, thinking isn't your strong point, none of you," said Leon with a smirk. "It's okay this time but don't let there be a next time." The smile became a frown and his eyes seemed to get darker with the implied threat. "Weren't you supposed to be in the kitchen too?" he asked, looking at Perro.

Perro glanced nervously from Leon to the stranger and wiped a froth of beer from his moustache. "I'll go right now," he said.

Leon shook his head and curled his lip in disgust. "Never mind. They aren't gonna do shit. Are you?"

Both women shook their heads and said nothing.

"Anyway, everything looks good," Martin said.

"Real good," said Leon, staring down Storm's top as she leaned forward to remove the plastic wrap over one of the trays of food. He smiled while he ran his tongue across dry lips.

"What's wrong?" Storm asked. "Missing your girlfriend?" She looked pointedly at Champagne, sitting in a chair beside the new man but with one leg draped across his thighs. "Oh no, that can't be right. You don't strike me as the champagne type. You're probably more into Kool Aid."

Silence can be staggering when it occurs suddenly. No one said a word after Storm's comment. Storm stood where she was acutely aware that she'd given up everything. Now Leon would know that she had seen the contents of the flash drive, that she knew the truth about him. One comment. One stupid comment and she'd put them all in danger. "Or Bud

Light, or herbal tea," she continued, trying desperately to deflect.

"Are you trying to say Leon's cheap," Martin asked. "I mean sure, he breathes through his nose to keep from wearing out his teeth, but that's not necessarily a bad trait."

For another moment the silence went on and then the new man laughed, laughed so hard he snorted, which set the others off. Even Lisa managed a chuckle and Storm was able to escape to the house.

Once in the kitchen she leaned back against the island and took deep calming breaths. A moment later her mother walked in.

"I'm an idiot. A moron," she told her mother.

"Stop," said Lisa. "We got through it. You're okay. We're okay."

CHAPTER EIGHTEEN

JOE CAME DOWNSTAIRS and entered the kitchen just as Leon walked in from the dining room.

"You have any peppers?" Leon asked no one in particular. "You know, those yellow things, come in a jar?"

"Pepperoncini's?" Lisa asked.

"Yeah, that's what they're called." He turned toward the open back door and shouted, "You guys need anything else?"

A chorus of "no's" and a "we're good," greeted his question.

"You two," he said, indicating Joe and Lisa, take them out to the table. He strode past them, stopping in front of Storm. "You," he said in a voice that was all command and no request. "I want to talk to you out here." He opened the french door and gestured for Storm to go first.

Storm held up her hand, silencing whatever her parents were going to say, then stepped through the doorway.

He followed and closed the door firmly behind them. Storm turned, arms crossed defiantly and asked, "What do you want?"

All pretense of civility gone, Leon's eyes glittered with malice. "Don't think I didn't get the snide comment," he said.

"What comment?" Storm asked, as if she had no idea what he was talking about.

"You know damn good and well," he countered. "That little remark about me wanting Kool Aid. I know you saw what's on those flash drives. You hung yourself and your family too. Not that you'd care. They locked up the wrong crazy bitch, didn't they?"

Storm tried to come up with a response, but her thoughts were moving in too many directions. Leon had more to say. "Your dad stole the box and then what, shared it with you and your mother, Jackie too? What, did you all sit around and watch it, pretending you didn't like it? That's how you self-righteous assholes operate. I'm used to that and I can deal with it, but pulling your shit around my boss, that I can't put up with."

"Your boss?" she said, and as the realization of what he'd said struck her, she saw, by the look of consternation that swept across Leon's face, that he'd revealed something he'd never planned to.

"I thought he was just someone who delivered messages for your boss in Pelican Bay, but he's not, is he?" Storm said. She didn't need to hear his answer because it was written right there on his face. "So, let me get this straight. Your boss isn't in prison, he works there."

Storm realized she had to get Martin and share this information. She started to turn away and Leon swung. She saw the blow coming and tried to duck but his fist struck the side of her head and slammed her back into the wood-paneled wall. She reacted as she did to most physical confrontations--aggressively.

She launched herself head first at Leon's midsection, throwing her arms around his waist and trying to find the gun she knew was holstered at the small of his back.

Twisting free, Leon smashed his elbow into her ribs. She staggered back into the wall, using it to keep her balance. Then she ran toward the door as Leon reached for his gun. He dragged it free, was raising it to take aim, when she banged through the french doors shoulder first and ran into the kitchen.

She got three running steps inside when Leon burst through the door behind her, the gun now leveled at her back. Her whole body tensed expecting the bullet he was about to unleash.

Storm stumbled past her father, barely aware of him, caught sight of her mother, who was right in the line of fire. Slapping her hands on the center island, she spun and kicked out at Leon. She had to stop him before he pulled the trigger.

As Leon ran past Joe, intent only on Storm, the knife in Joe's hand slashed forward. Momentum did the rest. The gun wavered and the muzzle dropped as Leon used his left hand to feel for the sudden sting in his neck. He brought his fingers away, looked at the thick dark blood dripping from them and his eyes went wide.

Storm watched as Leon dropped the gun, which hit the linoleum floor with a heavy thud, and put both hands to his throat. The pulsing red arc became a trickle, soaking into his shirt in a growing stain. He stared at Storm and she saw his face go pale. In moments his strength failed him and his hands loosened, allowing more arterial blood to burst forth.

He turned his head and stared at Joe, who still held the paring knife Storm had used to slice pickles.

Leon reached toward Joe, lost his balance and fell to his knees. It looked as if he were trying to say something, maybe call out to his men, but though his lips moved, no sound came out. He slid sideways, coming to rest on the floor near Storm, who stood there, one hand on the top of the center island for balance. She looked at her father in shock. Had that really happened?

Leon's blood, thrown in arcing patterns across cabinets and pooled on the white linoleum, turned the kitchen into a slaughterhouse, filling it with the dank copper smell of blood. For a moment the three of them froze in silent horror.

Joe stood with the paring knife still clenched in his hand. Lisa, who stood at the sink, was the first to react. "We have to get out of here," she said in a rough whisper. "We have to find Jackie. We have to get the hell out of here."

Before they had a chance to do anything, Perro stepped into the kitchen. When he saw the blood he drew his gun. Then he saw Leon's body.

"You," was all he said, as he raised his gun, aiming at Storm.

"No!" Lisa screamed, and threw herself between Storm and Perro. There was a loud bang as Perro fired. Storm's feet slipped in the blood on the floor. Someone grabbed the back of her shirt and began pulling her away.

"No!" she shouted and tried to break free. She turned to see who was holding her and realized it was her father. He tightened his grip and dragged her from the room. "No. Let me go," she demanded.

"Stop it," he said. "You can't do anything. I have to get you out of here. Stop fighting me." He tugged her farther into the entryway and toward the front door.

Jackie came running down the stairs, met them in the hallway, and shouted, "What was that? What's going on? Was that a gunshot?"

Startled, Joe loosened his grip, Storm broke loose and turned to Jackie, "Perro shot Mom," she said, panting and sobbing.

"Oh my God."

"Federal Agent. Don't move!" Martin's voice rang out.

Storm heard his command clearly but wasn't sure where it was coming from. Then came the loud bang bang of two shots so close together they had to be from different guns.

Storm and Jackie turned to run for the kitchen, giving up on his efforts to protect Storm, Joe followed.

Catching motion outside the kitchen window, Storm saw Perro ducking behind the raised garden bed. To hell with him.

Surprised to see her mother still standing, Storm raced to her, spun her around, and searched desperately for the wound. If she could find where her mother had been shot, stop the bleeding, maybe she could keep her alive until help came.

"He missed," Lisa said, and Storm could hardly believe it. Had to drag her eyes from the frantic search for blood to her mother's strangely calm eyes.

"How?" she asked, undisguised wonder in her voice.

"I have no idea," Lisa said, and shook her head.

"We have to go. Where are they? Where's Bud?" asked Joe.

"Upstairs, said Jackie breathlessly. He wasn't feeling so well. He's locked in the bathroom. I'll explain later."

"Perro ran out and he's hiding in the garden and I don't know where the rest are," said Lisa.

Storm having no patience for her father's questions decided to find out for herself. Creeping through the dining room she peered outside and saw no one. She wasn't fooled. She'd seen Perro sneaking behind one of the raised beds in the garden. The man who she had witnessed terrorizing defenseless dogs. The man she knew was peddling kiddy porn. The man who had tried to shoot her mother. As the images she associated with that man flooded her mind her rage exploded. As she ran across the deck, leapt down the stairs and slammed through the garden gate she was no longer an entirely logical human being.

Hearing her come, Perro jumped up from his hiding place, aimed and fired. The shot went so high and wide Storm almost laughed.

Her lack of reaction must have rattled him so much that Perro forgot his gun and started running. At least that was her best guess. When he reached the fence he dove under it, pushing the wire up and struggling for a moment until he broke free. Once on the other side he spun, gun in hand.

Still unwavering, Storm slid under the fence like she was sliding into home. Perro's mouth dropped open in utter shock. He took a step back then turned and ran as if his life depended on it.

When he reached a point midway between the house and the trees where his dogs were tied, something must have caught his attention because he turned his head to look.

Storm followed his gaze and saw a car fishtailing out of the driveway and onto the road. She could see that a man was driving and recognized Champagne in the passenger seat. She guessed the driver was the man Leon referred to as his boss. In a not unexpected show of disloyalty, it appeared they were leaving Perro and Bud behind.

At the edge of the driveway, Storm saw Martin desperately trying to kick start his motorcycle. She was relieved to see he was alive.

Perro unwavering, continued running full out down the sloping yard toward the white-barked trees.

Storm suspected he was going to the dogs for protection. When he reached them, he would likely free them, and they'd come after her.

Realizing she was no match for two vicious dogs and an armed man she slowed.

From the driveway came the roar of a bike starting, followed by the sound of gravel being thrown. Under these sounds Storm heard something else, a strange metallic scraping. The sounds drew her attention away from Perro. She looked toward the driveway in time to see the dog scrabbling out through the window of her car.

Once free, he ran to her, rubbing against her legs, tail wagging and barking with joy. Her legs tangled with his squirming body and she tripped, falling just as Perro fired another shot at her. Marty yipped at the sudden sharp noise of the gun and slunk back toward the car. Storm realized he could no sooner conquer his fear than she could conquer her anger.

Rolling onto her feet she had taken only two running steps when she saw Perro reach the trees and disappear from view. What could she use as a weapon? She frantically searched for a rock, a branch, anything to use against him, or the dogs, or whichever was first to came from the trees.

A scream filled the air and echoed across the lake. Storm froze. *What was that?* Then came another sobbing shriek. Then another.

No longer looking for a weapon, Storm drew closer to the tree line and those anguished sounds. Between Perro's screams she could hear the low but savage growls of the two dogs.

As she drew close enough to see them, the two white dogs, tense and straining against their chains. watched in frustration as their prey made its escape.

Storm thought the dog's mouths, painted red with blood, looked as if someone had painted clown faces on them. Their glistening red teeth turning them into a horror show version.

Perro, on hands and knees, appeared to be crawling toward her, but Storm didn't think he knew or cared that she was there. His head was down, blood dripping from his hair. As he approached he gave an anguished howl and raised his face. She saw that it was shredded like raw burger.

Inside his torn jeans, where his right calf should have been, was a stomach turning emptiness. He pulled himself a few more feet from the dogs and then collapsed, curling in on himself, shivering and whimpering.

She took the gun that was clenched in his hand away from him, released the magazine and saw there were six cartridges left. Storm decided not to waste a bullet on justice. She'd just let nature take its course. She wiped the gun on her pants, removing mud, grass, dog saliva and blood and marveled that the attack had been such a surprise he hadn't even thought to shoot the dogs.

Storm glanced at the house. They would make sure Bud couldn't get free. They'd be fine. She was free to pursue Martin. He was the real problem. The only one who had believed Lauren's story, if he was telling the truth.

Did Martin know the man he was following was the actual boss, as Leon have revealed to her, and not just someone who worked for him? Would sharing that information be enough of a trade to keep him from investigating her?

She asked herself that question as she headed toward the driveway and her car. Halfway there she remembered her car had been disabled. The only things running were the motorcycles and Perro's truck.

Perro's truck! Storm ran back across the lawn to Perro. One of the dogs gave a sharp bark, but only one, as she drew near. Perro was no longer moving but he'd turned onto his back and she could see his bony chest rise and fall. He was still alive and breathing but she wasn't going to make it her business to keep it that way.

She reached into his front pocket with two fingers and on the first try found his keys. They were attached to a key ring with a chrome bottle opener and the plastic figure of a bikini clad woman with the words Las Vegas on a sash. To notice such detail seemed surreal and Storm realized she was operating in a heightened state of awareness.

Marty was still sitting beside the car, and jumped up when she approached. She didn't really have time to deal with him, but still she swept him up, opened the back door of her car and tossed him onto the seat. "Stay," she commanded. She slammed the door and ran to Perro's truck.

Holding her breath, she inserted the key, and turned it. The truck started right up and she backed out. The tires chirped as the truck leapt from the gravel driveway to the asphalt road.

Heading north, in the direction the boss had taken, Storm floored the truck. It seemed odd to her that they were heading away from town. Maybe he thought hiding in the countryside was a better idea. Maybe he was meeting someone. Or maybe he just had a home in that direction. She had no idea. It didn't matter. All that mattered was that she catch up to him, and to Martin.

The truck slowly picked up speed. She reached a tight curve going too fast and the truck lurched into the oncoming lane. A dark blue pickup was coming straight at her. She stepped on the brakes and jerked the wheel to the right. The trucks slid past each other with only inches to spare. As soon as they were clear, the driver of the other truck held down his horn in righteous indignation. She couldn't blame him.

The road straightened a bit and then began to drop, bringing it closer to the level of the lake. As she slowed for the next curve a glint of metal caught her eye. She knew there was a small parking lot just off the road with an old boat ramp. Lisa told her it had been replaced by a better one on the other side of the lake. She'd said the old one was now mostly used by local kids coming to park and make out or smoke weed, but that was usually at night.

That knowledge made the shine of metal even more interesting. As she drew closer she slowed. Fresh dirt and skid marks marked the entrance to the lot. Taking a gamble, Storm wrenched the wheel to the right. The truck fishtailed in the deep gravel, but she got it straightened out and shot down the deeply rutted road, the truck clanging and rattling and loudly announcing her arrival.

Seeing no point in stealth after her noisy appearance, Storm sped down the short road between the sparse trees then abruptly into a wide parking area. Straight ahead she saw the car parked on a concrete boat ramp, nose down, its front bumper inches from the water. Martin's bike lay on its side right behind it.

Storm slammed on the brakes and the truck slid to a rocking stop, to the right and only inches from the bike. Dust and gravel pinged off both bike and car. Taking Perro's gun from the seat beside her, she held it out of sight just below the level of the open window.

Martin, who was standing on the passenger side of the car, with the door open, also held a gun. As he turned to look at Storm it never wavered from where he was aiming it directly at Champagne, who sat in the passenger seat.

Storm risked looking away from Martin long enough to try and locate the boss of the LOA. She didn't see him and wondered if he was slumped in the driver's seat, maybe dead. Glancing back at Champagne, Storm saw her dark red lips moving. Was she calling on Storm to help her?

Storm got out of the truck but kept the gun and much of herself hidden behind the door.

"What's going on here?" she asked Martin.

He looked at her with an expression she couldn't read then said, "You know what's going on. A little vigilante justice."

Storm took a quick sidestep that took her away from the truck and gave her room to aim, which she did, right at Martin. "Vigilantes don't kill innocent people," she told him.

"You don't get it," said Martin, keeping his gun on Champagne. "Blade's not the boss. This guy is. This is the guy, and these are the people who pay people to have sex with little kids, and then film it. Blade's just giving him access to his distribution network in exchange for a few perks. Hell, Storm, he's probably trading the use of the fucking LOA for Ramen Noodles."

"I know," said Storm. "Leon told me right before he tried to kill me. So, do what you were trained to do. Arrest them. Call in your guys and have them locked up like you promised."

"Why, so he can trade his way out?" asked Martin bitterly. "You know how it works. From what I've heard, you don't think so highly of our system of justice. Seems like you'd be happy."

As they'd been speaking Storm noticed, with her peripheral vision, that Champagne was easing her legs around so that she was sitting sideways. It would take only a second for her to jump out of the car and run. As soon as she did, Storm planned to shoot Martin.

"You aren't a good man," Storm told him. "You're too willing to kill."

"Is that the excuse? Is that the one you'll use to rationalize my death? You'll tell yourself it didn't have anything to do with me knowing about Lauren, knowing what you are. Will that make you feel better? Will you have even one sleepless night?"

"I haven't slept through a whole night since I was thirteen. Maybe I will after this. Maybe saving an innocent person will help me start—"

"Innocent," said Martin. "You think Champagne is innocent?"

"Just because she's a stripper or a porn star or something doesn't mean she's not a victim."

"Oh, for God's sake. Are you going to stand there and give me some feminist bullshit while holding a gun on me? I'm not going to kill her because she's some damn porn queen. I'm going to kill her, and him, because of my sister.

"My sister got off the boat from Cuba just in time to be "helped" by someone like them. I know that because they found her body two years later, pregnant and dead.

"I learned that she tried to escape multiple times, so often they got tired of dealing with her and sold her to someone making snuff films. After I became an agent I got ahold of the tape and watched some animal tie her up, put a plastic bag over her head and film it. You know how long it takes to die that way? A long, long time. She was fourteen."

"I'm sorry," Storm said, swallowing hard. "I'm sorry about your sister and about all the other kids but Champagne didn't kill your sister. She wasn't in those videos."

"No," Martin said, "She wasn't. But who do you think held the camera?"

Storm looked directly at Champagne for the first time since arriving. The look in her eyes told Storm all she needed.

Bang!

Champagne's body fell back into the car, the red soles of her high-heeled shoes like two exclamation marks. Storm dropped the gun to her side and walked up to stand beside Martin.

"The way you missed Perro, I didn't think you were much of a shot. Maybe I should have been holding my gun on you, not her," said Martin," with a smile.

"Which is exactly how you know it wasn't me that shot at him. I don't miss," Storm said, stubbornly refusing to fall into the trap of admitting that she'd shot at Perro.

"From the opposite side of the car, Storm heard a scuffling sound."

"Oh hell, he's not dead," said Martin. Storm followed him to the other side of the car and saw the man, who she only knew as the boss of the LOA, lying on the ground, pressing both hands against his chest. Blood was seeping between his fingers and turning the dust into dark mud.

Martin aimed his gun at the man's head, "This is for my sister, and all the other children you've hurt, you sick son of a bitch." He pulled the trigger.

Storm saw the man jerk and then go slack, his hands dropping from his chest, his eyes open but seeing nothing.

"We have to get you out of here," said Martin. "I better call this in soon or it will look hinky. I'll put Champagne in the car and we'll get our stories straight."

"It already looks hinky," said Storm. "Why did he drive down here? What was his plan?"

"I don't know for sure but I think he wanted to dump the car. He knew I'd seen it. I'm guessing he planned to hike until he found a car to steal."

Storm looked down at Champagne's feet. "Hike. In those heels?"

There was a short silence as they considered this and came to the same conclusion.

"She wasn't hiking out with him, was she?" Storm said.

"I think she was going in the lake. I'm betting he couldn't afford for he to be arrested. She didn't seem like the kind of person who'd have a problem turning on him.

Watching as he bent to lift Champagne's legs into the car, she said, "You need to know that I shot Champagne with Perro's gun."

He hesitated a moment then: "Good. That will make this easier. I can tell them that Perro was running for it. Leon had been stabbed and I had identified myself. He was frantic, running away from me, and waving at them to get their attention."

Storm realized he was thinking out loud.

"They saw him but ignored him," Martin continued. "That's when he pulled his gun and shot at them. They'll realize that one of his bullets hit Champagne. I then saw him running to his truck to leave and I made the decision to follow the boss.

If Perro shot at the car . . ." Storm ran the few steps to Perro's truck, turned. and put two bullets into the car's passenger door.

Bang.

Bang.

Martin nodded his approval.

"I just thought of something else," she said. "When I shot her, her blood must have splattered across the driver's seat. There's none of her blood on Leon. How are you going to explain that?"

"Shit," exclaimed Martin, "We have to dump the car. Help me push it into the lake. Hurry. The water will help confuse the evidence."

Martin put the car in neutral the two of them pushed. It was slow going at first and then the water began to trickle in. The added weight helped and the car gained momentum then slipped beneath the surface sending bubbles of air to the surface.

They watched for a moment then Martin barked, "You need to get out of here. Get back to the lodge and make sure everyone is on the same page.

Storm nodded, and ran to the truck.

CHAPTER NINETEEN

BY EVENING MIRROR LAKE lodge had been visited by two special agents of the FBI, the county sheriff, and an officer with the state police. Because of Martin's presence on the ongoing investigation, jurisdiction was shared between the county and the FBI. A special representative from Pelican Bay also arrived and the agents, including Martin's task force, took over the seating area and tables in the great room.

At first they had questioned each of them separately but now Storm, her family, and Jackie were relegated to the back deck, while Martin brought the LEOs up to speed.

As part of the investigation, Leon's body had been photographed, measured and removed by the local coroner's office.

Bud had been found deceased, sitting on a toilet in an upstairs bathroom, having died of an apparent heart attack.

One of the police officers found Perro, who had been horribly mauled by his dogs. He'd lost so much blood that if he survived it would probably be with profound brain damage. The two dogs were going to be held in quarantine to check for rabies and then would be put down. Storm's dog, was in her car.

"A popular breed," one of the cops had noted, but nothing more had been said about Marty.

The leader of the LOA, along with his associate, had been found where Martin had told them they would be. He had been shot once through the chest and once in the head. His companion had been shot once in the head. Her body had been recovered inside a car at the bottom of the lake.

Thanks to Martin's work, it was discovered that the leader of the LOA was not, as had been believed, the former leader, Blade. Rather, the current leader was Kent Hockamin, a corrections officer at Pelican Bay.

There was strong speculation that Hockamin had arranged to take over Blade's network in exchange for special treatment. That theory had yet to be proven but investigators had been assigned.

Everyone was questioned about what had happened at the lodge. Luckily, in the scant twenty minutes before law enforcement arrived, Storm and the rest had been able to rehearse the story she and Martin had concocted.

Part of their plan was to stay as close to the truth as possible. So, when it was her turn, it wasn't that hard for Storm to remember the version of reality she'd agreed to.

The two investigators wore suits, starched shirts and power ties. Both looked tired, serious and determined to find something in her story that didn't fit. They leaned forward, attending her every word. She would have to be careful.

"My father had been in prison for a long time, so when he showed up on my doorstep I was shocked. He told me he'd spoken with a woman who works for my mother and that she felt some of the guests were taking advantage of her."

Storm said her husband had been against her leaving but that she had left anyway. "My parents and I have been estranged for a long time, but I've always hoped we could get to know each other again. This seemed like a good way to begin."

"And why didn't you call the police?" the officers asked, as expected.

"Because we didn't know if there was anything to the story," Storm said. "By the time we realized there was, Martin, Mr. Perez, let me know he was with the FBI and asked me to leave."

"But you didn't."

"I did not," she agreed, and told him the reason, the same one she'd given Martin. That she and her father would stick around and make sure her mother was safe.

Then the questions about Leon's death began. As she replied Storm kept in mind how she'd been trained to write a narrative account after meeting with a client. It was important that narratives be emotionless and fact-based. She tried to keep her responses the same, but not so clinical she'd sound rehearsed.

"After I arrived and met the men, I knew Jackie was right. Something was off. It could have been my experience or training as a probation officer, or just a gut feeling, but the minute I saw them I knew they shouldn't be in my mother's home.

"When I told her what I thought, she made up a story about some friend in trouble with the LOA. She asked me not to call the police and put her friend in danger and I agreed to wait for a while. I didn't know then that it was me the men had threatened to hurt if she didn't cooperate.

"Eventually I found out the truth and she agreed to go to the police. That's when Mr. Perez revealed who he was and asked us to wait. He didn't think we were in any real danger, especially if we continued to treat the members of the club as guests. So that's what we did. The problem was they didn't want us here. They felt they could handle my mother and her assistant, but they wanted my father and I to leave. They hadn't expected us."

"So, it was your presence that precipitated the death of Leon Ray?"

"Not our presence. My nosiness. Someone dropped off a package. Leon kept it in his room and when I got a chance I took it. I opened it, found it contained flash drives and took one. Later I was able to view the contents.

My father was worried that I would get in trouble if they thought I'd taken the box, so he took it from me and put it back. They caught him doing that and thought he was the one who had taken it. Things escalated from there.

They took my phone and did something to our cars so we couldn't leave. It was terrifying," she said, for a moment losing her dispassionate tone. She didn't have to fake the shudder that swept through her.

"On Saturday his boss showed up, though we didn't know who he was at the time. While I was helping serve lunch, I said something about the drive, a sarcastic comment, and he realized I'd seen it. He was furious and came into the kitchen with a gun and shot at me. Surprisingly, he missed.

"My mother grabbed a knife off the counter and lunged at him, trying to keep him from shooting at me again. The knife hit an artery and he bled to death before we could stop it."

Storm looked down and paused a moment, as if composing herself, while she ran the story through her mind. Did she get it right? They knew the bullet they would find from Leon's wild shot in the kitchen, would serve as proof that Leon had been trying to kill her.

Lisa had convinced them she should be the one to take the blame for stabbing Leon. Joe had only been out of prison for a few days. Killing Leon could be a quick trip back. But a small woman, afraid for her daughter's life against a violent man with a record of crime, would be an object of sympathy. No DA would dare prosecute.

"We heard the car and the truck take off and thought they'd left. Then, we heard the truck come back but no one tried to come inside. Now we know it was Perro, come to retrieve his dogs. Those dogs were really vicious but still, attacking their owner, it's so shocking."

The group had decided that this story of Perro's return would explain why the engine of his truck was hot when law enforcement arrived.

"And where was Agent Perez in all this?"

"He was chasing them and he told us as he ran out that Bud was secured in an upstairs bathroom and not to let him out. Jackie felt bad. The two of them had become, sort of, friendly," Storm told them. "She thought he was a good man in bad company, but she promised us she wouldn't set him free.

Mr. Perez took off on a motorcycle to see if he could catch them. He told us to lock the doors and if anyone, other than the cops showed up, to call 911."

The investigation continued late into the evening, with different vehicles showing up, more police, the medical examiner, even curious neighbors. Everyone in the house was worn out, but eventually, after each of them had been interviewed several times, there was a sense of completion, even, if they were lucky, closure.

Storm could only hope they hadn't forgotten anything. Admitting that Jackie was sleeping with Bud had felt wrong. As if she were throwing her mother's loyal friend under the bus. But, it would explain any DNA the forensics team found. It might also help explain a heart attack and keep the ME from looking too closely. Because if they did, they would find the Antabuse that Jackie had been feeding him from day one. A kernel of information gained during the few minutes they were able to talk before the police arrived.

They left the lodge and moved to a local hotel in Crescent City, one where Martin and some of the task force had been staying. It wasn't the same hotel where Storm and her father had spent a night.

The five of them sat at a picnic table near the outdoor pool which was closed for the season. It provided a private place where they could talk.

Storm put her head down and let waves of exhaustion wash over her for a moment.

"What's going to happen to us?" Lisa asked, directing her question to Martin.

"Well, I believe you were told the forensic team had finished with the house, but they need to take a look at the yard where Perro was attacked. They should be releasing the lodge to you in a day or two. For now it's still a crime scene and they have to make sure no one is disturbing any evidence."

"I understand that," said Lisa. "That's not what I mean. I don't care about the lodge, or where I sleep. I want to know what will happen to us. Will we be charged with anything? That man died. Will we go to jail?"

"I'm not sure, but it would be very unlikely, at least if you stick with the story," he qualified. "Look, when they look at those flash drives and see what these people were doing . . . well people get into law enforcement for a reason and what's on those is . . . Let's just say no one will look at the four of you as anything but victims. Hell, you might even be considered heroes. My report will certainly back that up. I don't think any of you are in trouble."

Jackie sighed audibly. "I'm going to go to bed then. I'm so tired I'm seeing double. Lisa, how about you? Joe?"

"I'm with you said Lisa."

Joe also got up. "I guess us old folks are done for the night. Thank you, Martin, for all you did for us."

After they'd gone Storm turned back to Martin and said, "What about you? Are you going to be in the clear?"

He nodded. "I think so. I got a call an hour ago. They found a whole lot of cash and a fake passport in a toolbox in Hockamin's garage. Who knows what else they'll find.

"So, you're not in any trouble?" said Storm.

"Actually, I just talked to my office and was told that I'm being asked to work with the DOJ on a new program aimed at stopping human traffickers. I'll be working from our Arizona field office."

Storm sighed. It was over.

CHAPTER TWENTY

TO EVERYONE' SURPRISE, the lodge was released to Lisa the next day. They arrived that afternoon expecting to have a chance to unwind only to learn it was their responsibility to deal with the mess. They never mentioned this reality on television.

They spent the rest of the day removing all signs of the LOA. Joe dealt with the kitchen first, refusing to allow the rest of them into the room until it was sanitized. They were all too weary to argue and busied themselves removing beer bottles, cigarette butts and other debris left by the unwanted guests.

After a late dinner, everyone else had gone to bed. Storm, unable to sleep, left the house. She took Marty with her. The dog wanted a walk and she needed to think.

Although the bikers were no longer a threat, in a way, they had been a good distraction. Storm knew she had to deal with her other problems, ones that might be even more difficult to overcome. She was confused about the feelings she had for her parents. She was worried about her relationship with Tom. Her inability to reach him, to talk to him, was driving her crazy. Being so far away from her children, who were probably mad at her, or maybe even frightened by her sudden absence. It all made her life seem unbearable.

She wished Tom would answer his phone. She needed to tell him everything. How her mother, who had abandoned her at her worst moment, had been so heroic. How she'd jumped between her and Perro when he drew a gun. What was she to make of that? How her father had saved her life, attacking Leon when he surely would have killed her. How could he be the monster in whom she'd invested so much hate? Not for the first time, Storm wondered if she was the only real monster.

It was true her parents had made a lot of mistakes, done some incredibly thoughtless, even cruel things. Still, they were family. Maybe not much of a family when compared to Tom's, but that's what they were, and that meant something.

Marty tugged, nearly dragging Storm across the road to the familiar trail. The moon was full, and the ambient light was enough to see by, until they reached the darkness under the trees. Using the light in her phone, Storm navigated the trail until she reached the bench in the open meadow. Here she shut off the light and after a few moments her eyes adjusted and she was able to see well enough again.

She sat on the bench to think but Marty was bored, and he kept pulling at her and whining. Giving in, she unsnapped his leash and he dashed around the clearing, sniffing at everything, but staying in sight. Confident he would stay close, Storm was able to stare out at the lake and let her thoughts run free. So much to think about. So many loose ends. Martin knew too much. Would he really let her go? Could she face Tom and the kids finding out what she really was?

Her mother knew. Surely she didn't believe Storm's excuses for her late night activities. No one would. But she had pretended to buy it. Could she be trusted? Would she be able to survive another betrayal by her own mother.

Her father suspected. She'd done her best to convince him he was wrong but had she? Despite his declarations to everyone that his daughter was an innocent victim, he'd been there when she shot at

Perro. Innocent people didn't shoot people. Would he eventually realize that and betray her?

Most of all, why wasn't Tom calling? Had he and the children gone ahead, left her behind. The idea of another abandonment was too big to contemplate. The darkness of her thoughts carried her down, spiraling into a place of hopelessness.

Moonlight created a fairytale path that beckoned to her. It would be so easy to step forward and plunge into the lake. Let the water close over her as she drifted to the bottom and the peace and solitude that waited there.

Getting to her feet she crossed to the guard rail. Its white paint gave a luminous glow, an imitation of the moon. She stepped over it, reaching for the other side on tip toe then pulling her other leg over. Cautiously she moved to the edge of the cliff and looked down.

She thought about Martin and the two people they had killed, was it only yesterday? The man's name was Kent Hockamin. Champagne's real name was Susan Rains. Two new names to add to the growing list.

The toes of her shoes hung out just beyond the rocky edge of the cliff. Below and between them the lake sparkled as if millions of diamonds had been cast across the surface. They were so bright they made her eyes water. Or maybe those were tears. There was a lot to be sad about.

She was certain Tom had decided he'd had enough. She'd brought Howard into their lives. That darkly evil man. That alone would be enough, but then there'd been Lauren, maybe not evil, but damaged beyond all hope of redemption. Finally, she had done something that she understood all too well. She'd abandoned him, her children, and run off without them. No wonder he didn't answer the phone. Why would he?

Her eyes stung. She reached up to rub them and—

Crack!

The ground below her feet fell away and she was falling, dropping so fast she couldn't find the breath to scream. Her hands clawed at the dark and empty sky.

She hit the ground hip first and felt her bones move in ways they shouldn't. She rolled, a quick somersault and then a barrel roll, like the ones she'd do on the hill in the front yard when she was little. Over and over she'd roll down that gentle slope.

But there was nothing gentle about the craggy, nearly vertical wall she now tumbled down. Slowed by jagged brush that pierced her skin, skidding across loose shale, her arms pinned to her sides by momentum, she couldn't even brace herself for the moment she slammed into the water.

But it wasn't the water that stopped her descent, instead it was a rocky ledge that her flailing body crashed into. The air was knocked out of her as her ribs were compressed, some of them snapped, the jagged pain told her. When she finally drew in her first gulp of air the pain drew a sobbing moan from her lips.

She lay as quietly as she could, taking slow shallow breaths, while her mind scurried through an assessment of the damage. Sharp pain. That was her ribs. Dull throb, that was her right wrist pinned under her, both elbows, her right knee, her left leg. There was something funny with her left leg, but her mind shied from examining what.

She had come to rest on her stomach, head slightly lower than her body, between two boulders. They held her, wedged between them, kept her from falling into the lake, barely a yard below. The taste of blood filled her mouth. There wasn't much she could do. Maybe try to take her weight off her wrist? Her left arm seemed okay, a little ache maybe.

Okay, she had a plan. Step one was to free her right hand. Step two was to then use both hands to push herself slowly away from the edge.

The moon continued to give her a little ambient light, but it loved the lake and sparkled there reminding her of its presence. She knew she couldn't swim in this condition. If she fell into the water she'd die.

So, don't fall in.

Working her left hand under her chin she pressed against the ground, rolled slightly to the right and passed out. Somewhere within that peaceful, pain free sleep, she woke up and saw her father, his eyes filled with anxiety. But that was only a dream, he was locked up, far far away. She closed her eyes and the darkness wrapped its arms around her.

CHAPTER
TWENTY-ONE

THEY TOLD HER SHE screamed when they put her on the stretcher and strapped her in. That she screamed again as they dragged her up the side of the cliff. She didn't remember that, but maybe it was true.

Her throat was sore enough when she finally woke up. But maybe they had put a tube down her throat. She wasn't sure. Had no memory of it, but it would make sense. They had attached every other medical whatchamacallit to her. There was a needle in the back of her hand, with a tube that connected it to a bag of clear liquid hanging above her head. There was a thing she knew measured her oxygen level on her finger. Round patches with wires were glued to her chest. Her right arm and left leg were encased in plaster. She touched her face and found a band-aid across one eyebrow and when she ran her tongue inside her cheek she found a place torn by the sharp edges of her teeth.

"You're fine," Lisa said, pulling her chair close to the bed and looking down anxiously. There were dark circles under her eyes and each wrinkle seemed deeper than before. She reached for Storm's hand and then deflected, smoothing the sheet instead. "Do you remember what happened? You took Marty for a walk and got too close to the edge. You fell. Thank goodness Marty came back to the house dragging his leash, barking his head off. We followed him right to you. That's how we found you."

Storm wanted to ask about Marty but wasn't sure she was ready to speak. Her throat hurt. Her lips were dry and cracked. She needed water.

"You're fine," her mother repeated, speaking so quickly Storm could barely keep up. "Or, well I mean, you're going to be fine. The doctors say you were amazingly lucky. You broke your wrist and your leg and a couple of ribs. Your leg is going to take the longest to heal. I don't know if you remember, but they took you right into surgery and put pins in your leg and a metal plate. But they say it was a clean break and should heal just fine."

Storm saw that her mother's eyes were filled with tears and they were slowly sliding down her cheeks. She reached out, the cast on her wrist making the motion awkward, and patted the back of her mother's hand with cold fingers. "If I'm fine, why are you crying?" she asked, her voice rough and barely above a whisper.

Lisa leaned in to hear better, shrugged and offered a trembling smile. "You had us all scared. Plus, not much sleep last night."

"How long have I been here?" Storm asked. Her memories were jumbled and oddly uneven. She remembered being wheeled through a long hallway, light fixtures in the ceiling that seemed to jitter, sharp bolts of pain, too many people bending over her and then nothing.

"Since last night. It's about seven now, seven at night," she said, seeing Storm's confusion. "Not that long. You've been out of it most of the time, around twenty hours. A couple hours ago you woke up and the doctors came in and talked to you. Then, you fell back asleep. Don't you remember talking to them?"

Storm shook her head slowly and learned the motion made her head throb. Had she talked in her sleep, said something she shouldn't? Her mother said she talked to the doctors but she didn't remember that. What had she said? What had they said? Had she also talked to the police? No, the police had already questioned her. That was over. Her mother must have seen her bewilderment.

"You must be in shock," Lisa said. "You've been through a lot in such a short time. You had to deal with the bikers. You fell down a cliff. Now you've woken in a strange bed, in a strange room. But I promise you it's going to be okay. I just wish . . . I wish . . ."

Again, Storm watched as fresh tears washed down her mother's face. "Hey, stop that," she said, "you're getting me all wet." She hoped the humor she used to help her kids over rough spots worked equally well. Her mother grabbed a tissue, wiped her face, blew her nose and gave Storm a wan smile.

"I'm sorry. It's just that I was so worried I was going to lose you, and it feels like I just found you."

Now it was Storm's turn to tear up. She cleared her throat, fighting the loss of control. "You aren't going to lose me," she said reassuringly. "You and Joe, you're my parents and that's that."

"We should have been better at it."

Storm shrugged. After a lifetime of hating what they'd done she wasn't about to argue. Still, they were no longer those people.

Lisa poured water from a plastic pitcher into a plastic cup, added a bendy straw and held it to Storm's lips. Storm sipped at it, treasuring each icy drop as it slid down her parched throat.

"Do you think you'll ever be able to forgive and forget?" Lisa asked.

Storm thought about it for a moment. Then, her voice much improved said, "Forget? Probably not. Forgive? I think I'm already there."

Lisa burst into a fresh bout of tears, set the empty cup down, reached for the tissue box and put it on her lap. "Guess I'll just leave these here," she said.

"Probably a good idea," Storm agreed. "I have some questions for you. I want to know why you left."

Her mother stared into the middle distance, as if gathering her thoughts, then said, "I never wanted to leave you, you know. I didn't know what I was doing. After I saw what your father had done to you I had some kind of breakdown. I couldn't handle it. I left the house with nothing but the clothes I was wearing and my purse. It was like I wasn't in control of my own body."

"So where did you end up?"

"Well, at some point I misplaced my purse and what little money I'd had in it. A young woman at a bus stop was handing out flyers about a homeless shelter so I stayed there for a while. I worked in the kitchen and saved what I made. I went through the donations for clothes. It was a nice place run by good people, but I had itchy feet and didn't stay long. I was running, I guess, but didn't even realize it. I didn't think about you, or your dad, or anyone.

After I left there, I just kept moving. Each day was about survival and that took everything I had. I didn't have time or energy to dwell on why I was doing what I was doing. All I concentrated on was finding enough to eat and getting to another shelter, another place to run.

"It sounds terrible."

"It was, but it wasn't. It allowed me to escape the constant guilt that consumed me. I surrendered to insanity as a way to cope."

Storm shook her head. With her need for complete control, such a concession was nearly impossible to fathom.

Eventually, I ended up in a shelter in California. I didn't plan to stay long but they had a mental health program that I thought I'd try. I got to see a psychiatrist who put me on some medication. Between the antidepressants and working with a therapist I slowly started to do better.

After about three months I didn't want to run anymore. I felt strong enough to face it, so I got in touch with Aunt June. You were doing so well. Even though I wanted to be with you, I realized that was selfish. Coming back could disrupt your life and I didn't think I was well enough. I couldn't risk us getting close and then having to leave again. "Aunt

June and I talked about it and agreed that she'd continue to raise you until I felt I was ready. As time passed I just couldn't face you. I realized I didn't deserve to come back. I felt you would never forgive me. I know I've never forgiven myself."

This time Lisa didn't cry, instead she rubbed her fingers over her temples.

Storm realized how tired her mother must be, both physically, but mentally. She was exhausted too. It was a lot to take in at one time. Storm wanted to say something brilliant but instead she sighed and said, "You need a break. Maybe get something to eat. Why don't you get out of here. Let me get some rest?" Storm realized her mother wouldn't leave if it was only for her own sake.

"I guess, if you think I should."

"I do, now go, but come back with Jello. Not green." Storm waved her mother away, then winced as a fresh pain in her arm reminded her that she had tumbled down a cliff.

"Okay, but I'll be right back."

Alone, Storm relaxed into her pillow. Meds were wearing off, she realized. The half waking state was wearing away, the world getting brighter, edges sharper. The pain was waking as well, the throb in her head, the deep ache of bruises, the sharp stab of nerves reminding her she'd broken bones, torn tendons. It seemed a fair trade for the clarity of her thoughts.

Struggling to remember exactly what had happened took her back to the cliff.

She remembered standing at the edge staring down at the lake. Had she felt a strange compulsion to step forward? High places had sometimes done that too her, teased her to take the leap. But had she? She wasn't sure.

Her memory was foggy. She remembered some of the fall, the seemingly endless tumble, slammed around while rocketing downward as if she were on a runaway roller coaster. There was a moment of quiet in her memory, a moment when she seemed to stare down into a darkness that was more than just the lake at night. After that, a moment of piercing light, maybe a flashlight shone in her face? Then the hallway and the lights above. That was all. She knew there had to be more, and those black spots bothered her. Who had she talked to? What had she said?

The door swung open on its silent hinges but there was a change in the air and Storm looked toward it expecting to see her mother. Instead Joe stood there, his hand wrapped around the edge of the blond oak door, waiting.

"Come in," she said. Her voice was still low and a little rough. She knew he couldn't have heard her, but he stepped inside anyway.

"You feeling better?" he asked, as he crossed to the side of the bed. "Saw your mother in the hallway talking to the nurse. She said you were awake."

"I told her to get some rest and eat."

"I'm sure she'll get something after she's done grilling that nurse," Joe said.

"Hope so," Storm said. "Would you mind pouring me some water," she asked.

Her father took the plastic cup and pitcher and poured some water for her. He held the glass and directed the straw toward her lips as if he'd cared for the sick his whole life.

Again, she was struck by how wonderful water could be.

After she finished, he took the empty cup and set it back on the table.

"You want to try sitting up a little?"

Storm nodded and he took the controls and pressed a button. She felt the head of the bed slowly rise as fresh new pains rippled along her spine. Joe stopped the bed.

"You doing okay?"

"Yes, keep going. A little higher please."

He did as she asked, and she found she was ridiculously grateful.

"Could you hand me the phone? I need to call Tom."

Joe handed her the receiver and asked for the number. She recited it and he dialed. The phone range five times and went to voicemail. She handed the receiver back to him and he hung up.

"He isn't there, Storm said softly, aware that the pain of his absence was worse than the pain from the fall.

"I should have been there—you know—before," he said haltingly.

It took her a moment to understand what he meant. She was living in the moment, relishing the cool taste of water, the silly joy of sitting up in bed. He was in the past, reliving the fire.

"You should have," she told him, unwilling to let him think otherwise.

"I'm sorry," was all he said.

It was enough. Storm had already decided, though she hadn't even been aware of making the decision, that she would forgive—had forgiven—her parents. Their lives had meted out the justice they deserved. Her mother in homeless shelters, battling mental illness, separated from her family. Her father, in prison for decades, cut off from everyone he cared about. Yes, it was enough.

Storm closed her eyes for just a moment, but she must have fallen asleep, because when she opened them she saw her mother had returned. She'd put her gray hair up in a neat bun, washed her face, but she still looked exhausted. They both did. The two of them had taken the only chair, Joe sitting in the seat, her mother perched on the arm. They looked awkward and uncomfortable and it made Storm smile.

They saw and exchanged puzzled looks, which made Storm smile even more. "You guys look like two buzzards circling a carcass, not sure if it's dead or not."

"Oh my gosh, what a thing to say!" Lisa declared, but she also smiled.

"Well, she's your kid. What did you expect," teased Joe.

The door burst open wide and Storm's children ran into the room. Their arrival changed everything. The terrible white room, with its hushed tones and the constant beeping reminder that life is short, was suddenly transformed. It became filled with action and color, emotions of fear and fury and curiosity combined in one sticky, wonderful mess.

Startled, she sat up too quickly and pain slammed her back, made her go aspirin white and sweaty. Her mother took control, cautioning the children to be careful, then helping them.

Lindsey took her mother's hand and cried without restraint, each sob loud and dramatic and genuine. Joel climbed on his mother's bed, with a small assist from his grandfather, and despite Tom's admonishment, lay along her side, sucking his thumb as if he'd reverted from seven to two.

Storm pulled the children against her as best she could, savored the smell of Joel's SpongeBob shampoo and boy sweat. She used her fingertips to wipe away Lindsey's tears.

"I'm okay," she told them. "I know I look pretty awful but honest, I'm okay."

Joel shifted and the pain reminded her that she had broken ribs. It didn't matter. Nothing mattered but that they were here. Until that moment she hadn't realized that the entire week, since leaving her family to pursue this quest with her father, she'd only been partly alive. That she'd been as sterile as this room-- with a purpose--but without passion. As cold and mechanical as a gun.

Looking past her children, she saw Tom. Their eyes met and once again, just like the first time, she saw behind his eyes the promise of a resting place, the sanctuary that she needed.

Tom crossed to her, reached out to grasp her hand, but stopped short when he saw the needle embedded there. Instead he cupped her face gently, the only part of her body that wasn't bruised, battered or bandaged. Looking into her eyes with raw, unmasked emotion.

"I was so scared," he said. "When that woman at the lodge told me you were in the hospital. I was so frantic, she didn't want me to drive, especially with the kids in the car. She threatened to stand in front of the car if I didn't take a moment, calm down. She's fierce, that woman."

"That's Jackie," Storm and her mother said in unison. They both smiled.

"You sound good but you look terrible. Did you break every bone in your body?" he asked, trying but not quite managing to smile.

"She was lucky," Lisa answered for her.

"Yes, a boulder broke my fall," Storm said.

"I can see that. What else did it break. What did the doctor's say? When are they going to release you?"

Storm patted the back of his hand. "The doctor said I was going to recover. My leg is the worst but six weeks in a cast and I'll be able to start running again. Don't give me that look," she said. "You know I have to run. It's the only thing that keeps me sane. Six weeks without running. You're the one who has to live with me. Maybe you're the one people should be feeling sorry for. I mean, if we are still living together."

"Of course we're still living together. If you're willing to live with me. After you left all I could think about was how your leaving was affecting me. After several days of feeling sorry for myself, I realized I was being an ass. Of course you had to go help your mother. It's not like I didn't know you've wanted to see her for a long time. Or didn't understand how hard that would be for you. Then, suddenly, here was your chance and I didn't make it any easier for you.

He looked at them apologetically, then back at Storm. He reached up and smoothed an errant hair from her face, frowning at the band aid across her eyebrow.

"I'm sorry it took me so long to get here. Once I realized what a fool I was being, I knew I had to be with you. It took me longer than I wanted because I had to get someone to help out at the new office and hire movers. After that, we hit the road and we didn't stop for anything, well except the bathroom, right guys?"

The kids snickered at the reference to the bathroom, and that made Storm laugh. Tears ran down her face, but she didn't brush them away. The emotions that bubbled free were nothing she wanted to tamp down or hide. There was nothing about this feeling she wanted to contain.

When she was able to stop laughing and crying she clutched her side with her good arm and allowed her mother to wash her face with a cool cloth, while her father poured her more water.

"Kids, these are your grandparents, Joe and Lisa, I mean Grandma and Grandpa Dean. Joel immediately tried to climb over the rail to go visit his grandfather, so Tom helped him down. Storm breathed a sigh of relief to have the squirming weight off the bed, but immediately missed the warm presence. It was a perfect metaphor for her family.

"You really my grampa?" Joel demanded, standing in front of Joe in his ninja warrior stance.

"That's right," and this is your grandma," he said, indicating Lisa. "She lives near a lake. Isn't that cool?"

Joel seemed unsure, but finally nodded. "Yeah, I guess. Not super cool though."

"No probably not super cool," Joe agreed somberly.

"Have you kids had anything to eat?" Lisa asked. "There's a nice little cafeteria downstairs. They have hamburgers and chicken strips, all sorts of things. Chocolate milk too I think. That was always your mom's favorite."

"I like chocolate milk," Lindsey said, her now dry eyes going to her new grandmother.

"Should I take them downstairs and have them get something to eat?" Lisa asked, looking from Storm to Tom and back.

"I can go with you, help herd," Joe offered.

Tom looked to Storm for an answer. She nodded. It would be good to have some alone time with Tom, even a few minutes. Besides, after going through what they had at the lodge, she was not about to doubt her parents' good intentions.

"Yes, please take them. If they want to go, of course. Do you guys want to?"

"Yes. Yes. Yes," enthused Joel.

"I guess," said Lindsey, always the cautious one.

"Okay then," said Joe. "What do you think you'll want, a hamburger sure sounds good." Taking Joel's hand as if it were an old habit, Joe and his grandson walked side by side into the hall.

"I'm not sure I can find the elevator," said Lisa. "Do you remember how to get there?"

"I think so," Lindsey said and led the way.

When they were gone, Tom moved to the other side of the bed so that he could take Storm's good hand in his. He was careful not to disturb the needle taped there, gently entwining their fingers and sinking into the chair.

"Oh, Stormy, you had me so scared. Tell me it's all over and you're coming home."

Storm pulled her hand free, reached over the rails and gently touched the face she knew so well. "It's all over. I'm coming home."

CHAPTER TWENTY-TWO

IT WAS MARTIN WHO finally got Tom to leave the room, he could be persuasive, as Storm well knew.

"I just need to ask your wife a few more questions. After that you'll both be free to go. I know you'd like to get on with your lives."

"We would," Tom agreed.

Storm was amused by the hard stare Tom gave Martin. She'd never seen her husband take such a testosterone charged attitude. Normally, when she mentioned that some coworker or client had flirted with her, he'd laugh it off, joking that the poor guy must have been decimated when he realized how little chance he had. With Martin, although she'd never said a thing about him being interested, there was a definite edge. Not jealously, exactly, something more preemptive and slightly terrifying. Like two roosters facing off. Well, she was nobody's hen. They should both know that. She sighed.

"Go on. Go check on the kids. Get something to eat. I'm not going anywhere."

Once Tom left, Martin took the chair he'd vacated. "You okay?" he asked. "You look like shit."

"How nice."

"Sorry, that came out wrong. I meant to say, you look like warmed over shit."

He smiled, and Storm couldn't help but smile back, amused by his odd charm. He was dressed in a good suit, dark gray, with a red and gray striped tie. For the first time he actually looked like what he was.

But neither the smile nor the mood could last for long. This man held her secrets and her fate. True, she'd witnessed him kill a man. Put a bullet in his brain.

It didn't matter. He was FBI. She was a housewife and mom with a history of getting too close to people who end up dead. In court, if it was him against her, there'd be no contest over who they'd believe.

"Looks like we came out of this just fine. I wanted to let you know that. Blade is in solitary for his part in this. He'll be in solitary a good long time. Yeah, we're good . . ."

"But?" She knew he wanted to say something else. Something she didn't want to hear.

"The thing is," he said, "I'll be moving to the Arizona office and I'll be out in the field a lot. We cover a lot of territory. Since you're moving to New Mexico, which is pretty dang close. Well, I was thinking, from time to time it might be nice to have a partner who can operate a little left of center. You know, someone who isn't constrained to follow all the rules."

"You mean the way you are? I haven't seen much evidence of that?"

"Well," he said, and his cute crooked smile suddenly took on a much more sinister aspect. "You gotta do what you gotta do. I know *you* understand that."

His emphasis on you sent a chill down Storm's back.

"Don't look so freaked out. I'm not asking you to gun down anyone. I'm just saying, could be a time I'll need a little help, keeping an eye on someone, moving a little weight."

She knew by weight he meant body. "I don't think I can do that."

"Well, sure, not right now. You're all banged up. You've got drugs in you. Though probably not enough from the way your face is all scrunched up. But when you're feeling better. After you get moved and settled in and the boredom starts to settle . . ."

"My life is not boring," she snapped.

"Of course not. Didn't put that right. I meant to say, when you see someone get away with murder, or hurting someone, maybe some kid. When you see that again, and again. Well, I'll be in touch when you're ready."

"What if I'm never ready?" she asked, though she was afraid of his answer.

"Oh, you'll be ready," he said with a grin that held far too much confidence. "Trust me. Once you go down this road, once you feel that sense of balance and know you're the one responsible. Well, there's no high better than that. No substance more addictive. So, I'll leave you my card now. He took one from a metal case in an inside pocket of his suit and placed it on the table next to her pitcher of water. "I know you'll throw this one away. You'll convince yourself that your life is enough, for a while. So, I'll call you, every now and then and leave my number. Eventually, you'll call back."

"Get out," she said. She said it softly, calmly. "Get out."

"I'm going," he said. Standing, he paused, looked down at her. "We're going to have some good times together. When you're ready." Then he winked, gave her the full effect of his smile, smoothed his tie and left as he'd promised.

"Monster," she said. But she said it in a whisper. You never want the monster to hear you say its name.

CHAPTER TWENTY-THREE

LISA AND JOE RETURNED first. "Tom and the kids are visiting the gift shop," Joe explained. "Lindsey insisted. She's something, that one."

"They're wonderful children," Lisa said, "smart and thoughtful."

"Yeah, they can be," Storm agreed. "You know, I think calling you by your first names might confuse the kids. Would you mind if I call you Mom and Dad from now on? Especially when they're around?" Storm saw her father's throat working, her mother's eyes blinking rapidly.

"That would be fine," her mother said. Her father nodded, gave her a tight, controlled smile.

"Good," said Storm. "I'm glad that's settled."

There was a light tap on the door, then it swung open and a heavy-set nurse with gold braids, a radiant smile and pink scrubs entered, carrying a tray.

"Bet you'd like a little pain relief, wouldn't you, sweetie?"

Not waiting for an answer, she moved swiftly to the bed, ignoring everyone but her patient. She handed Storm a tiny paper cup with three pills then without wasted motion, pivoted to the side table, poured a cup of water and handed it to her. Storm swallowed the bitter trio gratefully.

"I'm Barbara, your night nurse," the nurse said. "You're sweating, and your hands are shaking. You're in a good amount of pain, and you don't have to be. Next time, you press the call button. She put the device, which had been dangling from the side of the bed, under Storm's good hand."

"I didn't want to fall asleep," Storm explained defensively. "I wanted to see my family."

"Your family can wait. I'm sure they wouldn't mind." She glanced at Lisa and Joe but it was such a cursory look that neither responded. "Now, I'm going to lower your bed and dim the lights. I want you to get some rest. Visiting hours are over at eight, so about ten minutes." Again, she glanced at Storm's parents, and again didn't wait for a reply. In this room it was all about Storm's wishes.

Storm couldn't completely suppress her smile. A bossy nurse who had your back was not the worst thing.

"We should go," said Lisa, earning a smile from Nurse Barbara as she left to tend to others. "I'll be back tomorrow though."

"We both will," said Joe.

"And then you'll come back to the lodge and stay until you're well enough to travel."

Storm hadn't thought of where she would go after leaving the hospital, but as her pain receded and a dreamy wave that felt like a call to sleep swept over her she yawned and said, "I'd like that." Then, remembering something she added, "But Joe, I mean dad, aren't you heading to Mexico?"

"Well, not just yet. First, I'm going to hang out here a few weeks, make sure you're fine and help your mom with some things around the place. Maybe build that deck she was going on about. You know, the one on the front so folks can sit out and look at the lake?"

"Sure," said Storm, stifling another yawn. "But I thought she couldn't afford it."

"I couldn't," said Lisa, "until Joe pointed out that I actually own forty acres of timberland. He thinks we should be able to sell off some of the trees."

"Sell some. Cut some," said Joe. Should be able to mill enough that after a bit, a year or two, we can use it to build that deck, maybe fix up a few other things."

"A year or two," Storm said, startled enough to throw off the drug induced fog. "You two aren't getting back together?"

"Oh, heavens no," Lisa said. "That ship sailed a long time ago. We just realized that we used to like each other for one reason or another, and those reasons are still there. We just didn't like each other in a way that made for a good marriage."

"Thank God," said Storm, her head sinking back into her pillow.

"I realized that Father Anthony always said we should help ourselves, become our better selves before we could help anyone else. I have a lot to make up for. Maybe helping your mom and Jackie is a good start."

"You okay with this?" Storm asked her mother.

"Free labor? Heck, yes," she said, "Jackie would shoot me if I said no. I made her a partner in the lodge. I've been meaning to tell you. After the risks she took for me, for us," she said, wrapping her fingers around Storm's wrist so as not to touch the needle still lodged in the back of her hand. "I realized she was just as much family as any of us. Besides, the lodge saved me. I'm hoping that having a place that's her own will save her too."

"That's a kind thing to do, Mom," Storm said.

Lisa squeezed her wrist. Was about to say something when once again the door was opened, and Tom, Lindsey and Joel trooped in. With them, claws scrabbling across the tile, came Marty, pulling on his leash and panting. His tail was shaking back and forth so fast his whole body swayed.

"What the heck?" said Storm, as Tom barely kept Marty from jumping onto the bed.

"We took him for a walk but as soon as he finished he made a beeline for the hospital. It was like he knew you were here. It was impossible to hold him back, right kids?"

Storm wrinkled her nose at the idea of Tom being unable to control a forty-pound dog. "Are you trying to teach my children to lie to me, Tom McKenzie?"

"Now Stormy."

Just then Marty stood on his hind legs, poked his muzzle through the metal bars and licked Storm's arm. "Goofy thing," she said, using the edge of her hand to stroke his whiskery face. Apparently appeased, he dropped to his feet then sat down, his tail still wagging as steadily as a metronome.

"Nurse Barbara is going to kill you," she warned Tom.

"Can we keep him, Mom?"

"Can we?" asked Tom. "Your parents told me if it hadn't been for him they'd have never found you. He saved your life."

"But Tom," she said softly. "He was abused, trained to be vicious. He wasn't very good at it, but that doesn't mean he won't one day attack the children. We can't take that risk."

"Look at him," Stormy. "Just look."

Storm looked down and saw both kids sitting on the floor. Marty was sprawled half on top, half under them. She watched as Joel took one of the bedraggled ears and tugged—hard. Her heart nearly stopped as she watched Marty turn his big head toward Joel's face. She was reaching for the bed rail so as to catapult herself to her son's defense, when Marty licked Joel's forehead, then dropped his head onto the boy's shoulder with a deep sigh.

"It's not his fault he wasn't treated right. But look at him. No matter what life did to try and make him a monster, it failed. He's a good dog and after what he did for you he's earned my trust. Of course, the kids love him to pieces. I'll bet he'd defend them to the death. In fact, I wish he'd been around when that Kline character showed up."

Storm thought of Howard, and of Lauren. Twisted, damaged people. She had thought they were like her, or that she was like them. Maybe she was, but maybe she didn't have to stay that way.

"I guess, maybe. Maybe he can stay. He's a real good ..."

The pills won, and she faded into a deep, dreamless sleep.

The alarm went off. Time to go to work.

Storm fought to wake up. It was like swimming through vast amounts of chocolate pudding, thick and dark. Like dinner last night. When they woke her to check her vitals and feed her more sleeping pills, and pudding.

The alarm again. But not an alarm. The sound went on too long, more buzz than jangle. No, not an alarm, a phone. The phone in her room. Finally, she was awake. The lights in the room were still dim. It must be early. Who would call so early? Were the kids okay?

The phone sat on the table beside her bed. On the right side. "Damn," she cursed as she rolled slowly onto her right side, the cast getting in her way, making it an awkward, lurching motion. Luckily, they had taken the needle out of her hand at that last waking. She was able to reach the phone and drag it from its cradle.

"Hello?"

"Hi," said a voice she recognized immediately. Martin.

"Hope it's not too early. Figured they wouldn't let you sleep much past six anyway. Not in any hospital I've been in."

"What do you want?"

"Just checking that you're alright. Are you?"

"Yes, I'm fine. I should be out of here soon. Maybe even today."

"Good. Glad to hear it."

"Great. Is that it then?"

"Well, hardly. I did tell you I'd call right? That I wanted you to have my number? I assume you don't have my card anymore?"

Storm remembered taking his card after he'd left and tearing it into the smallest pieces she could manage. She'd left the little pile of it on the rolling table they'd served her food on. She remembered wishing for a match, so she could burn the damn pieces, but of course, the sprinklers coming on would have been annoying. Someone had taken them away while she slept. Probably tossed them in the garbage or a recycling bin. She didn't think that was enough, and now she was sure of it. Martin was a curse not easily broken.

"I have your card," she said. "I'll call you when I'm ready."

"You're a terrible liar. I'm actually astonished you've gotten away with so much for so long. You've obviously had some help but you're going to need more. My number is—"

Storm rolled to her side and slammed the phone down. It hurt, but it was so worth it.

Rolling onto her back, she sighed, and stared blindly at the ceiling. The past was the past and she wasn't going back. She had carried so much anger for so long that she'd had to invent fictions to contain it all. It had driven her to cross lines that no sane person would, allowing her to become a vigilante. She'd been remorseless, even sadistically cruel in her pursuit of vengeance and justice. It had become the core of who she thought she was. But no more. None of it had made her happy or brought her peace.

In fact, when she examined it with brutal honesty, she had to admit that the justice killings had brought no balance to the world. The abusers were still out there, hurting the helpless, preying on the innocent. Life offers us many roles to play. Being a vigilante was only one of them. It was past time to remember that she was someone's wife, someone's mother, someone's child. That was enough.

Wasn't it?

ABOUT THE AUTHOR

Pamela Cowan writes mystery and suspense novels set in the Pacific Northwest. Her short fiction has been published in magazines and anthologies and read on radio. Cowan has worked as an audio producer, a magazine editor, and in the probation and parole side of criminal justice.

She has two grown children and lives with her husband and a number of four-legged roommates in Oregon, where she is currently working on a new series, *The L&M Detective Agency*, think buddy movie, sibling rivalry and murder, all rolled up into one.

Please visit my website at pamelacowan.com to sign up for early notice of new releases, contests and giveaways. If you enjoyed this book please consider taking the time to leave a review.

Thank you,

Pamela Cowan

READ EXCERPT OF COLD KILL
by
Pamela Cowan

She was a small girl but she put up a hell of a fight. Chuck gave her credit for that. He'd had to hit her twice with the blackjack—the leather-clad club he preferred—to get her to stop kicking at him.

His recruit division commander at Great Lakes, the Navy's boot camp, would have called her gutsy and that wasn't a term the old bastard used often. Chuck had busted his ass trying to impress the man, but he'd never been called gutsy.

Well that had been a long time ago. No use replaying old Navy shit. There was enough new shit to deal with.

Though that was true, the many habits Chuck had acquired in the Navy were still with him. He kept his once blond, now mostly gray, hair cut high and tight. He kept his shirts and slacks starched and ironed. He walked with his shoulders back, his head up, his spine straight and despite recently hitting the big six five, he worked hard to stay fit.

He ran three to five miles each morning and followed up each run with twenty minutes of old-fashioned calisthenics. These habits served him well. Some of the women he'd had to deal with could be a handful.

This one sure had been, but not anymore. She was lying at his feet, her limbs twitching uncontrollably, her lips opening and closing while she made a funny thin sound. She reminded him of a fish out of water, flopping around like that. He hoped he hadn't brain damaged her. He'd tried to be careful, tapped her lightly right on that sweet spot above the ear, but you never knew, the brain was a funny thing.

He bent over and pulled off her shoes. Good, no more kicking. He reached into the van and grabbed the five-gallon paint bucket. It was heavy, but he lifted it out without straining. He pried off the lid. The bucket held nothing but tap water. He lifted it high, then tipped the contents over the girl, drenching her clothes and sending the smell of wet dust to his nostrils.

He nodded. The buckets had been a good idea. Anyone nosing around the van would think they held paint. That would make more sense than a bunch of jugs of water. Making sense was important. Blending in, nothing out of the ordinary, that was the key. He was an angry man sure, but also a smart man.

www.ingramcontent.com/pod-product-compliance
Lightning Source LLC
Chambersburg PA
CBHW032154190626
46814CB00005BA/1982